RALEIGH REVIEW
LITERARY & ARTS MAGAZINE

VOL. 14.2
FALL 2024

RALEIGH REVIEW

VOL. 14.2 FALL 2024

PUBLISHER
Rob Greene

EDITOR-IN-CHIEF
Landon Houle

FICTION EDITOR
Jessica Pitchford

POETRY EDITOR
Leah Poole Osowski

EDITORIAL STAFF / FICTION
Dailihana Alfonseca, Alex Bryan,
Chas Carey, Kelly McCorkendale,
Robert McCready, Jeff McLaughlin,
Allison Frase Reavis,
Matthew Turbeville

BOARD OF DIRECTORS
Joseph Millar, Chairman
Dorianne Laux, Vice Chair
Landon Houle, Member
Bryce Emley, Member
Will Badger, Member
Tyree Daye, Member
Rob Greene, Member

ASSISTANT FICTION EDITORS
Erin Osborne, Shel Senai

SENIOR COPYEDITOR
Elaina Ellis

COPYEDITOR
Charlene Pierce

EDITORIAL STAFF / POETRY
Chelsea Harlan, D. Eric Parkison,
Sam Piccone, Melanie Tafejian

SOCIAL MEDIA COORDINATOR
Maggie Busch

ILLUSTRATOR
Nora Beers Kelly

LAYOUT & PAGE DESIGN
Alexis Olson

LITERARY PUBLISHING PROGRAM
Alexander Gast

Raleigh Review, Vol. 14, No. 2, Fall 2024
Copyright © 2024 by *Raleigh Review*

Raleigh Review founded as *RIG Poetry*
February 21, 2010 | Robert Ian Greene

Cover image "Tether" by Jan LaPerle
Cover design by Alexis Olson

ISBN: 978-1-59498-186-9

Distributed by Fernwood Press, an imprint of Barclay Press, Newberg, OR

Raleigh Review, PO Box 6725, Raleigh, NC 27628
Visit: raleighreview.org

RALEIGH REVIEW

table of contents

poetry cont. ——————————

RALEIGH REVIEW

VOL. 14.2 FALL 2024

FROM THE EDITOR

SNAKES HAVE BEEN COMING UP a lot for me lately.

It started with my mom sending me a text message with no text, just a photograph. It's a strange photograph, taken at night and from a distance. The subject of the photo is at the center of a spotlight, giving the edges of the picture that dimming vignette quality. If the photo were a little less exposed, not quite so harsh, the lighting might be described as nostalgic, maybe even romantic.

I hold the phone close to my face, then far away trying to figure out what's actually in the picture. At first, I think it's a busted cherry sucker with a twisted stick, that white cardboard tube I can remember pretending to smoke and then chewing to a pulp. I'm already thinking that a picture of a broken sucker is sort of artsy, and I start to imagine what the photographer might want me to take from this image. But then I remember: a story Mom told me a few days before about someone she knows and the recent killing of a snake. This is no lollipop thrown from a parade float and left smashed in the street. This is no photographer's statement on the dashing of innocence. Or, on second thought, maybe it *is* just that, this rattlesnake shot dead, belly up on a hot night in rural, drought-stricken Texas. Something lost. Ruined.

Yikes, I text back. Gruesome.

Depending on where you live, it might seem strange for people to take (and share) pictures of dead snakes, but it's a pretty common practice where I grew up. I remember drugstore bulletin boards of curling photographs, mostly men but some women and children too, holding up giant catfish and bass, deer and boars, bobcats and turkeys, and yes, snakes as long or longer than the braggart's own body. I'll spare you the gory details of these pictures, but know that while our mothers waited on yet another round of antibiotics sure to cure our strep throats, I, and probably every kid like me, studied these photographs with a kind of pensive fascination warped to near hallucination by the dizzying haze of childhood fevers.

We could debate the ethics of modern-day hunting, but I know where I stand, and you probably do too. It's the photographs that interest me now, the certain sense of pride, the reflective eyeball, the broad-smiled gleam of human teeth. I've never been in a picture quite like that, but I guess I participate in my own way. Just this morning, on my walk around the neighborhood, I spotted a snakeskin between the sidewalk and the fence. It wasn't enough just to see it. I needed a picture of it. I could have taken a selfie, could have held the skin up to show it came down to my knees. But I didn't. My photo is more like the one Mom sent me, although I guess you could say mine is more about the living than the dead, evidence of a creature that slithers on, that very well might have been watching me from a crepe myrtle branch as I studied what it left behind.

I know this will almost seem unbelievable in the way that coincidences necessarily do, but I'll tell you anyway and ask you to trust me on it. A good friend emailed me yesterday. She said she had a dream about me, that in this dream, I had the power to transform (you guessed it!) into a snake. But as a snake, I needed monitoring. She offered to watch me, and of course, I got away.

My friend and I agreed the dream was strange, but on second thought, what is an odd dream? What makes a dream regular?

"Ordinary dreams" is a phrase in my favorite sentence of this year's winner of the Laux & Millar Poetry Prize, Andrew Payton's "Descalzo." The lines in their entirety read: "Somewhere in the middle of life / I too confront the impossibility / of ordinary dreams" (34-36). The more I think about these lines, the more I absorb them in different ways, and I'm filled with wonder at the implications. One is the notion that perhaps at some point, we leave behind the dreams of our youth. Maybe it's our dreams as in goals and ambitions, desires. But maybe it's literal (is this the right term?) dreams too—the "forgotten pants" or "the inability to scream" kind of dreams. That at a certain point, those nightmares, sort of routine and dull when you think about it, become impossible, and we must confront something bigger, something so much more magical and perhaps even more real. Maybe there's some truth to that, whether the dreams happen when we're asleep or awake.

I've got an old dictionary of dreams book, one of those paperbacks that's more than 600 yellowed pages. As you might imagine, there are a number of listings for snakes, but none of them quite fit my friend's dream. In my snake form, I didn't bite anyone, for example, and my friend didn't step on me while bathing. (Some of these dream dictionary entries are strangely specific.)

In the dream, after I'd changed into a snake, I ran (or slithered) away. But after a frantic search, my friend found me, and even though there were people in the dream that wanted me dead, she, with the help of some of our other friends, helped me escape. She woke up before we succeeded or failed at our mission, but we agreed we must have gotten away.

Most of the dream dictionary's entries on snakes aren't exactly positive, but if you ask me, my friend's dream was about friendship, about searching for someone you care about and helping them even when it's dangerous.

As mentioned, we are pleased to bring you the winner of this year's Laux & Millar Poetry Prize, Andrew Payton's "Descalzo," as well as work by our contest finalists, John Mulcare, Mary Ann Samyn, and Sonya Schneider. Here, too, you'll find our favorite fiction pieces from this round of submissions and illustrations by Nora Beers Kelly, all designed and beautifully presented by Al Olson.

I guess you could say every issue of *Raleigh Review* is sort of like our own drugstore bulletin board. See us now, grinning from ear to ear, holding out to you what makes us most proud. Except, these poems, stories, and works of art are very much alive and more than well. The work here will live long after us, and that's why we do what we do. That's the spark you see in our eyes.

We hope you enjoy this issue, friendsssssss....

Until next time,

Landon Houle, editor-in-chief

JR SOLONCHE

MONOSYLLABIC

The best ones are the small ones,
those you need to hold in your hand
two or three at a time, those you need
to feel for size, and shape, and heft,
the blunt, the sharp, the smooth,
the rough, the square, the round,
the firm, the soft, the ones like rocks,
like bricks or stones in streams,
the ones like clods of soil or clumps
of clay, the ones you pile to build
the whole world with, and then
the ones you hurl to bring it down.

FLORA FIELD

THE YEAR GRANNY DIDN'T SPEAK

The cows' black and white spines
creep above the hedge—

I listen for their low bleats. And
because she doesn't

speak, we do things.
Hang the laundry,

buy braided jewelry.
She is silent

for few things—
just my mother

leaving England,
and the dead baby.

And supposedly,
there was the year

when the not speaking
did not cease.

Granny sitting there,
watching the stiff cotton

waft, and bleach,
in the paling sun.

THE LEFT AND RIGHT
ENDLESS FLICKERING

There is so much decomposition
inside of me I'd like to see language
again I'd like to be a woman
in the middle of thought
I thought poetry disclosed
what happened to me
when I was a child
when I was a daughter
but it just left me there
to be a daughter is to lay
yourself bare on the cold blue tile
curl up against the yellow towel
sit down in the light of what is leaving
so I lay down in that light

DAFYDD MCVEIGH

CARSEN

I HAD BEEN SPENDING AFTERNOONS at Rachel's house for three weeks before I realized her neighbors had no children. No real children, that is, just Carsen—though how *real* Carsen was eventually became a point of terrible contention between us.

I first learned this fact by seeing Carsen's waxy face up close; Rachel never bothered to warn me about it beforehand. The neighbor woman, Brianna, brought him by one day while the two of us were out on the porch, sipping lemonade. Rachel had snuck some of her mother's vodka into hers, but I wasn't brave enough yet to accept any in mine. I was drinking plain lemonade with my head hanging down in it, as if lemonade were something to be ashamed of. That sour, filmy aftertaste. It made me feel like such a little kid.

But right, I was talking about Brianna—standing there with greasy ropes of brown hair plastered to her mousy little head. She said, balancing that baby-like thing in a blue and gray blanket on her hip, "You girls don't know if the mailman's been by already, do you?"

I looked to Rachel, because I didn't live there and didn't feel like I had the authority to answer, even though I knew the mail had come. Rachel brought it in right after we got back from school.

She didn't look up from her phone. When I think of her today, I always recall Rachel as thoughtless and beautiful, not always unkind but emphatically disinterested in the lives of others. She said, "He was by about an hour ago."

"Shit," Brianna said.

Rachel continued looking at her phone and didn't say anything else. She, too, had long and stringy brown hair, but she wore it well, in a way that was youthful and carefree. A little reminiscent of Kate Moss. Brianna, on the other hand, did not look like Kate Moss. I asked her then, when the silence began to hurt my chest, "were you expecting something?"

"Oh. Yeah, just a package. I thought it was gonna come today, but there's nothing." She rocked Carsen then, in a way that struck me as both automatic and deeply tender.

"Sucks," Rachel said, "maybe it will come tomorrow."

Brianna twisted her lip. She was wearing some kind of tinted gloss, I noticed, and the wrong color of foundation caked into her wide pores. At that point, it had been a few years since I'd tried with makeup; I observed her hack job of it a bit fondly. "Maybe," she said, but she didn't seem confident.

"What's your baby's name?" I asked her, and Rachel rolled her eyes.

Brianna's face illuminated, as if I had activated her. "His name's Carsen. Spelled with an e, not an o. It's a Scottish name."

"That's a nice name. Is he asleep?"

She lifted him up to her face, peeked behind his blanket-shawl, and shook her head. "No, he's awake. He's just very well behaved. Did you want to say hello?"

This was when Rachel's lip curled into an evil little smile; she finally looked up from her phone. "Yes, S. You should hold him. He's very sweet."

When I remember the first time I held Carsen, I am still shocked by how heavy he was. Making those dolls, I've learned since, is quite an undertaking. His body was filled with something uncannily organic—something that felt like real human flesh. I only realized it wasn't an actual baby only because of its unnatural stillness. But even then, he looked to me more like an infant corpse than a doll. I was struck with the same kind of revulsion I would get from looking at roadkill, intestines spilling out onto asphalt, little raccoon face still intact.

Brianna, perhaps noticing that I was repulsed, said hastily, "Oh, he's not a real baby, by the way. He's a reborn doll. Do you know those? I know it seems weird."

"Oh!" I said with a relieved laugh, "He's a doll!"

"Yes, I'm sorry. I should've said that before. He's just very real to me, is the thing. Or, not really. I don't think he's real, *haha*." (She said that aloud, haha.) "But I just forget it's weird is all."

"I don't think it's weird. He looks very sweet. He looks very real to me, too."

It was then, I think, that Brianna and I became friends. See, she put her whole self in my arms, and I had been gentle with it.

IT WAS THAT SAME AFTERNOON I told Rachel I was probably transgender, and that someday I was going to transition. My whole body was shaking as I said it out loud, and she still didn't bother looking up from her phone. She was the first person I ever told that to. I was as relieved as I was insulted that it made so little of an impression on her.

The first thing she said about it, picking at her jagged nails: "Like, you're gonna do all that now?"

"Um. I mean, no. Probably after we graduate." But back then, even naming it, let alone making concrete plans for the upheaval of my entire life, felt so big that it could consume me. How she had the audacity to reduce it all immediately to logistics still amazes me.

"Okay. That's cool. You should do it, then. Live your life. I hope it makes you happy."

"I think it will. Maybe."

She added then, "I mean, I'm not into that. Like, you know. I didn't—"

"Yeah. I know."

"No, I just mean, I didn't know how long you wanted this thing to last between us. Once you go on T or whatever. I'm not into that."

How like her, to assume that my investment in our fledgling relationship was any greater than hers. Secretly, I had begun harboring the belief that I wasn't bisexual at all, and that I had 'come out' all too hastily. Now that I'm older, I only date men. But to admit it to myself at that point would've been to call myself a straight girl—that is, to relinquish my tentative claim to queerness. And that, at least to me, was completely untenable. "You can still call me a girl. And S. I don't have anything else I want you to call me yet."

"Alright. Well. I hope it all goes well for you. Seems like a headache to me, all that just to be a man of all things. But good luck with it."

I look back at that moment now and see the two of us in that basement, her father's football paraphernalia lining the walls like some sort of Packers cathedral. This obscene confession booth. She joined me on the couch, and we watched a comedy movie that was mindless, raunchy, and ultimately more embarrassing than it was funny. I look at myself now in that room and I see my face as if it were in the middle of a water damaged photograph.

MY MOTHER USED TO SAY during those months I was with Rachel how lucky I was to have such a nice girlfriend. She meant it in the way older women talk about their *girlfriends,* their friends who are girls. The concept of sex or romance was so unthinkable that there was no need to even clarify. Today I actually think it's funny, how bad I was at playing lesbian that even my paranoid mother couldn't smell anything between us but chaste, female friendship.

My parents both worked late hours, so I went to Rachel's most days rather than go home alone to scrape together dinner and eat by myself. My father was a truck driver, and my mother was a nurse. I was their only child, and they doted on me whenever they had the time, though that wasn't often. My parents, too, were curious, ambitious people in their precious free time, my father an armchair philosopher and my mother an avid consumer of all things Greek and Roman history.

In that way, Rachel's parents were completely alien to me. They lived in an expensive but cheaply made McMansion that was decorated in that gauche, faux-rustic style. They had a single bookshelf in the living room filled with unopened clothbound classic novels. I think the both of them, Rachel's mom and dad, did something related to real estate. Both of them embraced me tepidly and with great suspicion. Unlike my parents, who saw Rachel sparingly and took her for this wonderful friend of mine, her parents seemed more keenly aware of the mismatch between us, though they weren't able to put their finger on quite what it was (since, of course, Rachel was not yet out to her parents). They treated me not like Rachel's friend or girlfriend, but like one of her indulgences. The useless plastic toy their beloved child had insisted upon.

There was one night where Rachel's father—a small man whose balding pattern made it look like he was wearing a Roman laurel—grilled me about where I had learned to use a knife. According to him, I had been clutching it in my hand like a caveman as I tried to cut into an overcooked slab of beef. He taught me then, with simmering impatience, how to cut meat with a knife and fork, while Rachel and her mother looked on silently. Such hot, terrible shame. Sometimes when he said grace, I would pray on my own (even though I didn't believe in God) that he, too, would be made to feel very stupid someday.

I deduced soon enough that Brianna's husband was another one of those incurious suburban brutes who seemed to emerge fully formed out of Indiana soil. He came home every day at 5:30 PM, give or take twenty minutes, and did so always in a blustering huff, as if his day was so hard, his life so important. I was seventeen then and already found it comical, the idea that someone like him was living a life with any real stakes. He was tall and broad and a little pudgy, someone who looked like he used to play high school football but didn't anymore. I watched him from Rachel's window sometimes and felt that if I poked him with a needle, he might pop.

Brianna spoke of him with deep reverence, but no fondness. And this, before our fights about Carsen, was the first real disagreement between Rachel and me: I would often invite Brianna to sit with us on the porch. I never learned exactly how old Brianna was, but she was certainly somewhere in her mid to late twenties. That is, someone well outside the age bracket of an acceptable friend for Rachel and me. I was keenly aware of that, and invited her anyway. Now, when I remember those afternoons with her, she morphs into a teenager just like us.

She said on a day in mid-October that was bright and humid, like it was pretending to be July, "Did you know some scientists say that we're living in a simulation?"

Rachel laughed, but I tried to humor her. "Oh, do they really?" I asked, but I knew no scientists were saying that so simply and earnestly, not any serious ones.

She nodded eagerly, bouncing Carsen in her arms. "It's true. Some of them say they've proved it."

"Where'd you hear that?" Rachel asked.

"I read it somewhere. I forget where."

"Facebook," Rachel half-muttered to me.

"It was an article someone posted. It was a real article." She shushed Carsen, even though he was a doll and was not fussing. In some ways, Brianna reminded me of my parents—intelligent but uneducated people, who shared Brianna's tendency to latch onto bogus information they read online. Though there was no way Rachel could've meant this, I felt her condescension toward Brianna as a rejection of something fundamental in me as well.

"That's interesting, though," I said, then fixing my eyes on Carsen's stiff, tinted pink lips. "Do you think it matters if we are or aren't?"

"What? Of course I think it matters," Brianna said.

"Does it, though? If we're just alive either way?"

"Who said I'm alive?" Rachel interjected. She looked at me and added, "The accident was ten years ago, S. You have to let me go."

"Ha," I replied flatly.

Brianna ignored her, either not understanding the joke or too fixated on her line of conversation to care about it. "It matters to me. Maybe not in my day-to-day life, but I can't think living in a simulation just wouldn't *matter*." She rocked Carsen aggressively then, so much that I was scared. As if some real harm might have come to him.

RACHEL THEORIZED that the whole thing with Carsen was because Brianna couldn't have children, or because she wouldn't be able to handle the responsibility of a real baby. That is, she attributed a quality of *lacking* to Carsen. But I saw immediately how infinite Carsen really was. It's not that Carsen didn't need Brianna like a real child would; it was that her imagined Carsen would never not need her, and he would never need her in a way that was difficult or complicated. He was a vessel that could be endlessly invented and endlessly adored.

"I mean it," Rachel said in that godawful basement—she was raising her voice because her parents weren't home yet and she had nobody bigger to be afraid of. "*Stop* inviting her over to chat with us. Or at least stop humoring her about that stupid doll. It's … it's not good for her brain."

"She doesn't think he's a real baby, though. She told me he was a doll."

"She doesn't act like she knows that. She's just fucking weird, okay?"

"That's not a crime, though. To be weird." It was then that I remember staring at a faded decal of Brett Favre and becoming acutely aware of my posture, the breasts protruding from my body and my nipples brushing against the rough polyester of my shirt. I felt the urge to peel off all my clothes, then my skin. I wanted to peel back layers of muscle and fat like phyllo dough until I was nothing. It was like every single part of me was too soft.

"I'm not *saying* it's a crime. I just don't want to have to talk to her. I don't want to look at that ugly doll anymore."

I sat there still thinking about my breasts in my shirt, and I felt like I was living a life with some sort of film over it. A life that would never progress, never bloom into anything. "Okay," I said, and I imagined I was a TV dinner, sitting still at the back of a freezer.

BECAUSE RACHEL HAD MADE HER STANCE CLEAR, some days I went over to Brianna's on my own for an hour or two after school. This, funny enough, just made Rachel even more angry at me, but I couldn't help it. I liked Brianna, and I liked her awful fake baby.

The whole fire thing that happened later probably shouldn't have come to me as a surprise. Brianna had extension cords plugged into extension cords in every room of that house, as if consequences for reckless actions were just things that happened in movies, not real life. On one side of the front hallway, she had a framed, faded print of Van Gogh's *Sunflowers*. A parallel bouquet of cords sprawled underneath it.

She said one day in her living room, which was built so eerily like Rachel's, "You never wear any makeup. You're sort of a tomboy, aren't you?"

"I guess so."

"You're really pretty, though."

Even though I had a complicated relationship with being 'pretty,' I was flattered. Her words came from a place of uncomplicated kindness.

My mother pushing me toward femininity felt more urgent than this, a little more desperate and forceful. Brianna's kindness did not feel like coercion.

She was changing Carsen on a little side table, with real disposable diapers. It was something I clocked as wasteful immediately, but I couldn't bring myself to pass real judgment on it. I watched her throw a clean Pamper in a little trash can and pull out another one to put on her baby doll, who was incapable of soiling it. I knew she would throw this one away as well, and another and another, indefinitely. For a moment, Carsen and his implications felt absolutely gigantic to me.

"I'll try it, then. Maybe for the winter dance."

"Oh, you shouldn't wait for that. You could just throw a little lipstick on in the morning, some mascara. It would look really good." She picked Carsen up then and began patting his back to burp him. I thought both things were true at once, that my femininity was ultimately a lost cause, and that I would start wearing mascara to school. Because even then, when I knew I would come out, would transition and become unacceptable to many people in the very near future, I could not shake my long-standing preoccupation with being good. That terrible, intangible state of being. Good classwork for my teachers, good daughter for my parents, good girlfriend to Rachel, who I didn't even like very much.

I sat there watching Brianna, and I had the singular urge to live a completely unjustifiable life. I wanted to feel no shame for my body and for the way I held a knife. Brianna asked if I wanted to hold him, and I did; yes, of course I did.

When I held him, I felt love for him. It was a love as big as any I have ever felt.

I HAVEN'T TALKED TO RACHEL IN A WHILE, but I hope she's doing well. I heard recently she's gone on to study business so she can do the same thing as her parents. I imagine her there, hating it but physically unable to conceive of anything bigger for herself.

The night of the fire was the last time I stayed over at Rachel's, though we'd been slowly petering out for a few weeks before that point. It was clear that Rachel had realized the only thing we had in common was that we were girls who liked girls—though even that, at least on my end, was dubious. It's just that neither of us knew how to break up with someone and couldn't even conceive of that as being something that people did. It was another one of those things—those real life things—that seemed to only happen to TV characters.

I think the real catalyst, though it's a little hard to place exactly, was Rachel's father. He yelled at her one night when he got home from work, a purple vein comically popping out on his forehead. She had gotten a D+ on her calculus test, which he saw while checking her grades online. Her mother watched the whole episode passively, chewing on her lip.

I knew already that Rachel's father was a terrible, short-sighted man. What shocked me about the episode was that he went on his tirade in front of me—either I was finally integrated enough into the family tableau that he did not feel like he had to hide the extent of his wrath anymore, or else I was just not worth the effort of keeping up appearances. I am almost certain it was the latter. The whole time it was happening, Rachel kept looking past him and meeting my eyes. As if I was catching her in the act of stealing from me.

Later, in the basement, she told me without any preface, "I'm sorry if I was mean to you when you came out to me. Or dismissive, whatever." She was trying to affect that air of apathy she always had, but her voice was shaking so badly I was embarrassed for her.

"You weren't. We don't have to talk about it."

"Okay," she said. Rachel could be inconsiderate, but I knew that when I first became her friend. I saw no reason to resent her for being exactly as she was. "And you should probably stop coming around so often. Once a week or so is still fine. But I think my dad thinks we're dating."

"Well, we are."

"You know how it is with him, though. Don't make this a whole thing."

"Yeah. I know. I won't make it a thing."

She wasn't officially breaking up with me, but she was breaking up with me a little. I knew it like she knew it, and I felt no great loss.

I THINK IT WAS A TUESDAY when Brianna's house finally went up. It was in the early evening, right before dinner. We all went outside in case it spread to the other houses, but it didn't get to us, and somehow I knew it wouldn't. On Rachel's front lawn, I felt not like an evacuee, but like a voyeur.

Sharp flames cleaved through the cluttered rooms of that house. Watching this rapid, senseless consumption bordered the sublime. There was a moment there where I almost did believe in a higher power. I had not realized that something as banal as a suburban homestead could be destroyed so completely and so fantastically.

Her husband wasn't home yet, but by the time we'd all made it outside, Brianna was already there, waiting on the lawn and shivering without a coat. She looked so frail to me then, almost herself like a doll. In the excitement it took me several minutes to realize she did not have Carsen, that she had left him in the burning house. This realization came to me, so cruel and sudden and heavy, that I thought I would drop it.

Brianna noticed me staring, and only shook her head. I ran across the lawn to her, ignoring the screaming of Rachel's father. He had neither the will nor the authority to punish me—but more importantly, I wouldn't have cared if he did.

"He's not a real baby," Brianna said quickly, as soon as I touched her arm. "It's okay. I'm okay. It's not a real baby." Though there in her self-consolation, I saw the paradox that needles at me to this day. If only he were real, she would've had an excuse to run in and get him. But of course, if he were a real baby, he wouldn't have been her Carsen. ◆

JOSEPH MILLS
THE YADKIN

IT WAS THE KIND OF DAY that was so beautiful it was almost painful, although none of them would've put it in terms like that. That would've been weird. They didn't talk about beauty, pain, anything abstract or much of anything at all. Instead, the three of them had simply agreed it was a good day to cut class when one of them said, "River?" and the other two nodded. They would deal with their parents later if they ever found out, which they probably wouldn't. They took Johnny's Chevy and threw a couple of old tire tubes in the back. One of them had a long nozzle that would scrape your side if you weren't careful, so they would use that one to float the beers they took from the fridge Ed's dad had in the garage. The sky was a cloudless blue. Some said a Carolina blue. They didn't think about it in that way because they weren't going to Chapel Hill or any college. They knew they were going to end up at the factory, if they didn't do a stint in the Army first, and that was fine with them. It had been a good job for their parents, one that put a refrigerator dedicated wholly to beer in the garage. It was going to be a good job for them.

Johnny had cigarettes that he shared with Ed. They had always been around cigarettes; it paid for the fridges, and there was a time when they didn't smoke and then they did. They couldn't have pinpointed the exact moment. They would have just been in some group when a pack was passed around, and they took one. What Johnny didn't admit was that he liked Marlboros, a betrayal in a town dominated by RJR, so he would

transfer those cigarettes which he would buy in Virginia into soft Camel packs and then destroy the recognizable red and white boxes.

The only person who didn't smoke now was Hank. His mother said it would stunt his growth, and he said he believed her even though they pointed out there were plenty of tall people who smoke. Hank said probably they were tall first and then started, but that wasn't true. Hank's mother said only idiots smoked, but she didn't work at the factory. She worked at the hospital. It was a favorite word of hers. Idiots. People who smoked. People who rode motorcycles. People who bought things on credit. Basically, everyone they knew. They didn't hold it against Hank. His mother was just his mother. They were sure if she heard about them cutting school, they would be idiots. And maybe they were. But it was good to be on the Yadkin. Fall in the air. The water carrying them along. By the Interstate, in a farmer's field, they could see the huge confederate flag. It would always be there. There would always be a job at RJR. They would always be young. Idiots. But that was fine.

It took a while for Johnny to realize that Ed wasn't with them anymore. He looked back up river and saw him standing waist-deep, shouting and gesturing. It took Johnny and Hank a while to get back up to him. He had gotten out of his tube and somehow had gotten his foot wedged under a rock. It was twisted around, and he couldn't get any leverage to get out. By the time they got him loose, the sky had grown dark, you couldn't see the flag anymore, and Johnny realized that his cigarettes had floated off. ◆

HAN VANDERHART

PARTIAL LISTING OF MY KINKS

Kindness. The red flowering bee balm.
The coach who offered both their hands
to me, lying on the gym floor. Twice. Oh and
the usuals: fingers and silicone, leather and
rings. Nipple clamps. Us being penitential
with each other. When I opened my arms to
you, yesterday, and you looked at me, entered
them. Hope. Which is like, sometimes, a stick
with feathers, filling the body with anticipated
life. The white and purple morning glories
appearing in the yard. The flowering dill. Not
making it to the end of the movie. Losing our
clothes, the children asleep upstairs. Any deep
kindness. Any small kindness. The person who
has come through a great pain, or is still there.
The opening of my chest to them, not violently,
but like the flowers at the top of the mountain mint.
Oh my deep heart. My shallow body. Feeling
yours lift into me through your clothing.

NOVGOROD IS A THOUSAND-YEAR-OLD CITY WHOSE NAME MEANS NEW

In front of the stone cathedral
of St. Sophia, I remember

a woman resting her hips
on a man's as he lay
in the grass and the clover

and that the sun was setting
and that I had to look away.

AMANDA RABADUEX

PEE-WEE HERMAN COMES TO MY 40TH BIRTHDAY PARTY

Sun uninvited. Shining orange glow of prescription bottle on my nightstand. The day came too soon. But once balloons were filled, I resigned myself to the secondhand of the watch. I watered the plants. He showed up in his gray suit and red bow tie. The word of the day was *satisfied*. We cut the cake, scooped ice cream, tried to dance, but we never screamed. Until the talking chair and the genie's head and the flowers singing on the windowsill, how could I have realized? I want so much less. Connect the dots, la la la. So much more. Boys and girls, why don't you take a picture — it will last longer. Boys and girls, I know you are, but what am I? What am I, now?

KELLY TERWILLIGER

CARROT

I've eaten all the carrots now
except the one with legs
and the one with a funny kink
that bends out and around
whatever isn't there anymore.
How does a color like this exist
underground? Once
I made a carrot costume for a little boy.
Skinny orange body
and a frill of green on a green-brown cap.
I found the orange sheath just the other day.
Small carrot skin resurfaced
from another time. Who needs it now?
Who but me
would know what it is?
Secretly, I folded it.
Secretly, I put it aside.
You can stay with me, I said, *a little longer.*
What else is there to say.
Carrots in the underworld.
Carrots pulled to light.

TOM GILBOY

WHIPSNAKE

NOTHING IN THE REARVIEW, nothing ahead. Traffic out here at four in the morning a rarity.

Minnesota State Patrol Sergeant Karl Kohlhardt pulled over to the shoulder and parked. He checked mirrors again, switched off lights and ignition, and pressed a pair of panels on his chest until they chirruped, confirming he'd disabled the infrared and muted the mic. His body cam was live but registering nothing. He put on his trooper hat, squared it, and waited for his eyes to adjust to the darkness, his imagination to the silence.

On clear nights, the strip of highway through the miles of red pine was the parting of a dark sea. Tonight, under a slab of October overcast, it was a drainage ditch, or an open-ended grave a man might lie in forever, staring up at nothing, not even stars.

Sergeant Kohlhardt touched two fingers to the rim of his hat. At academy he'd been advised by his field training officer and mentor to find a means of practicing greater vigilance over certain mental processes. A detective, he was told, could afford flights of fancy. Not so much a patrolman with no backup inside a twenty-minute window.

He patched the radio to siren speaker, stepped from his unit, and walked out to the center stripe. The road's vanishing points east and west were hidden by puffs of pale mist a couple of miles off. They looked like spider egg sacs. Sergeant Kohlhardt tapped the rim of his hat.

Around and behind his unit, he opened the cargo hatch. From under a trauma kit, a defibrillator pack, and a teddy bear issued for the comfort of children in crisis, he pulled out a vintage rosewood submachine gun case. He undid its leather straps, again looked up and down the road, released the catch and raised the lid. From its cradle of red velvet, he carefully lifted out the silver B-flat English cornet.

Carrying the little horn in the crook of his arm, mouthpiece warming in his palm, he walked back along the white gravel shoulder to an x of slightly darker stones. It marked the spot where a month ago he'd stopped to drag a doe off the road, and where, as he stood over her contemplating her frozen stare, a spit of radio static from the siren speaker broke the silence like a gunshot.

The echoes answering each other had propagated into a clatter that went on and on, coursing up and down the corridor. This softened to a rhythmic whisking, as if brushed by the pines, making him think of maracas, as it dissolved finally over the treetops.

Astonished, not a little spooked, he'd clapped three times sharp. Within seconds, dozens of bony birds had murmurated overhead, passing above repeatedly as if trying to find their way. Their clacking ripened to a clopping like castanets by the time they lifted off above the forest.

Wondering whether the freak acoustics had to do with the walls of pines or the ruled line of asphalt or all of it together, he'd whistled the first bars of "Will o' the Wisp," and long after the last of it faded in the distance like the sustained high keys on a piano, he remained still.

Then he'd laughed, hooted really, and was treated to something like hundreds of barred owls banked deep in the woods.

The following night, Sergeant Kohlhardt had come back with the horn. And every Monday, Tuesday, and Friday shift since, he'd devoted his lunch breaks at three-thirty in the morning to uncovering the sounds he'd always suspected were in the little instrument. These eleven sessions with the trees had taught him more about timing, listening, and the shaping of his mouth than years of schooling and private lessons. They offered direct access to the mystery, and they hinted he could find the answers for himself. They reminded him of the nights in the months he and his wife were first married.

Sergeant Kohlhardt sighted the bell southeast and across the road at the venue's sweet spot, one of the fine-needled tamaracks that here and there elbowed their way out of the pines. He exhaled, waited, and then filled his belly and chest.

The siren speaker spit.

Elvie from Tribal Services came on. Sergeant Kohlhardt shipped the horn to listen. She had cows that had broke fence north of Cloquet township to lay claim to the warm road. Sandi at Pokegama Dispatch picked up. "I have Karl westbound on two-two east of Pokegama."

"No, we're good. I've got this." Elvie cut out, and Sergeant Kohlhardt breathed warmth over the mouthpiece while the reverberations of the voices, like stadium babble, broke up over the trees.

Leaving behind a thrumming.

It didn't fade. The vibrating undertone seemed to grow louder. It didn't come from the siren speaker. He turned in place to get a fix on it. It was a horizon sound, like the shudder of a distant train gearing up for a hill. But the nearest line was fifteen miles north of Hibbing.

It clarified to the rumble of a combustion engine, a big one, tuned to an indulgent gurgle. He wondered if he was hearing twelve cylinders or if this too was a phenomenon of the trees.

East, the ball of mist had taken on a yellow glow. It brightened like a bonfire being fed, and two shimmering pinpoints formed. When the headlights broke through, he looked away. Incandescents, but intense, maybe aircraft lamps for the lumens they put out. He squinted into them long enough to see they were big-dished like truck lights, though markedly close together. They lit up everything along the roadway. The gravel shoulders gleamed, and the tamaracks in the dark pines shimmered as if going up in flame.

He estimated the driver to be doing ninety at least in a posted sixty-five.

Willing himself not to break into a run, Sergeant Kohlhardt made for his unit, until hearing the keen of a supercharger, the driver putting the pedal down. He ran and climbed in and set the horn on the passenger seat. He kept an eye in his rearview, and when he judged he was nearly visible to the driver, with a fond smile he engaged his strobes.

The driver did not let up, not one bit.

Before him Sergeant Kohlhardt watched his unit's shadow on the white shoulder shrink down like a dog or a child about to get hit. In the last second, he remembered to activate his body cam.

The car shot by like a leaping fish.

He kicked on his high beams.

It was a classic, one of the big roadmasters from the thirties. A beauty, with the glistening beige-pink finish no one did anymore. He clipped on his mic and restored the dashcam link. Pulling out he told Sandi he was in pursuit, and of what, and why.

"How fast?" said Sandi.

"Those old cars were dynamos." Already the little oblong taillights were barely stars. "We're at mile four-three westbound."

"Heading into Whipsnake."

"Yup." Sergeant Kohlhardt lay his hat over the cornet to keep it from rolling.

STATE 22, an otherwise thirty-mile straight shot from Duluth to Poke-gama City, features midway a six-mile spasm of asphalt known to locals as Whipsnake. Since 1931, this section of roadway has served as testament to the Minnesota Division of Highways' ill-starred efforts to address the consequences of one of the more dramatic upheavals of the last ice age, when a tiny rogue glacier broke away from the main pack to run wild for the better part of a millennium. Whipsnake is a fever dream of roll-ercoaster dips and rises interspersed with bobsled curves, five of which tilt at angles exceeding U.S. highway standards. It is generally held that the middle four miles presents the densest concentration of yellow-di-amond hazard signs in North America. Human nature being what it is, from the day this stretch first opened to traffic, drivers have risked their lives trying to establish the record for fastest point-to-point from one end to the other. Sergeant Kohlhardt couldn't count the number of times he'd been first on the scene.

He was within a quarter mile of the big car as it closed on the first of the challenges, Rabid Otter, an S-curve slaloming two mud lakes. Here pickups and sport utilities rolled all the time. He flipped on the siren, air horn, yelp, and wail. The driver didn't touch his brakes as he entered the first bend, straddling the double yellow. Sergeant Kohlhardt's speedometer read seventy-seven, and he let up, and the other car took off. Who'd risk that with such a car? Was it stolen? Was it some kid?

Another glimpse before it entered the second, tighter bend, rear wheels skipping. Sergeant Kohlhardt held his breath waiting for the drift that would take the car into the trees. But the driver held firm, as if he knew the turn and knew his car. In the apex of the curve, Sergeant Kohlhardt felt his inbound wheels lift, and his nerve slipped. He tapped the brakes. Next he was off the shoulder sliding through thicket, to halt upright, pine boughs mashing the passenger side. He cursed softly, and hitting the gas, sprayed bramble and needles.

Shooting out of Otter he saw the other car a half mile on. It was pulling away. He looked down and saw he was at one hundred and five.

He neither gained nor lost through Candy Ribbon, a battery of crests and troughs all but folding over each other. It was as he rose from the last foggy dip that he saw the car's brake lights flash just before it ran over something big and blue in the road. Then it was in his beams. A blue builder's tarp spread across both lanes, or cans of blue paint fallen off a truck, exploded on the pavement. It was under him, gone.

And he thought no more about it. Because here Whipsnake unkinked for a quarter mile as if composing itself for The Neckties, and it was here the driver, instead of gunning it down the straight, was electing to pull over: brake lights again, sustained, as the car moved half onto the shoulder and came to a full stop.

Sergeant Kohlhardt drew up behind. He doused the sirens, though his adrenaline kept on ringing. He unsnapped his sidearm holster, set the emergency brake, and turned on the unit spotlight. He swiveled it onto the car.

An eyeful. From the rear, with its bulbous trunk section and two tiny high rear windows, it resembled the nose section of an airliner. Under the trunk handle, a chrome script badge read *Pierce*. Hearing music, he lowered his window an inch. Big band, loud. A horn section with its hands full trying to keep up with the singer, a gal with a peppery vibrato having all the fun.

The brake lights remained on. The car was still in gear. The driver might take off.

Mounted above the left taillight was a pumpkin-orange license plate. He called it in.

"Restate make please," said Sandi. "Restate tag."

"Make is Pierce-Arrow. Tag is Minnesota seven-nine-oh-two-six."

"You broke up. Restate tag."

"Tag is just five digits. It's a 1938 plate. Contacting driver now." He aimed the spot through the rear windows and saw the top crescent of an ivory steering wheel. No passengers.

No driver.

The driver presumably having ducked down out of sight. Sergeant Kohlhardt unlocked his shotgun and took it from its mount.

Then he noticed twenty feet ahead of the old car, in its headlights, another blue patch. It covered the roadway edge to edge. It looked like a big round sidewalk-chalk drawing of a flower. When he'd come this way at twelve-thirty it hadn't been here. Nor had the first blue patch.

He peered into the dark of the pines feeling unreal to the moment, to himself. He'd about made up his mind to call for backup, when behind the steering wheel a head popped up.

It was an elderly woman with short wispy duckling hair. What he'd taken for a steering knob on the wheel was a yellowed arthritic hand. Her head swayed slightly with the music. And even with the strobes going full tilt she didn't so much as consult her mirrors or turn and look back. She peered ahead through the steering wheel, the top of which was level with the crown of her head. Impossible she could be the driver. Though her hand was on the wheel.

He deliberated before returning the shotgun to its rack. He grabbed the flashlight and got out with one hand for his sidearm. He shone the beam into the woods on either side. Far back in the trees the blackness went on forever.

The tune began to skip, the singer and the horns butting the same wall over and over. The old woman leaned over the passenger seat, and the music stopped. Then it picked up again, as if she'd replaced the needle on a record.

The needle on a record on a turntable beside her in the car.

She patted the back of her head, maybe at a coiffure long gone. She'd yet to acknowledge his presence. He wondered if she knew he was there. He walked slow, and as a courtesy, he paused in the spot's beam to not give her a heart attack when he appeared at her window.

When she peeled out, the rear tires kicked up stones, one clipping Sergeant Kohlhardt between the eyebrows.

How long was it before he realized the car was gone, that he'd been staring at a huge carnation on the road, of azures and dark blues, purple streaks, white highlights. It was well done, he thought, and it must have taken someone a long time. He felt ants running down either side of his nose and swiped at them and found blood.

Back behind the wheel, he tore citation forms from a pad and pressed them to the gash. His fingers were numb. In the rearview, his pupils were great big, and he thought of the spaces between the trees. "Hypovolemic shock," he said out loud.

Dispatch was speaking so he must have called it in. Elvie was on her way down. Sergeant Kohlhardt pictured the old car barreling into Pokegama City at a hundred and thirty, and he told Sandi to tell Elvie to put out spike strips, and hearing himself he knew she'd never be in time.

He set out full throttle, dabbing his forehead.

He didn't see the car until he was out of the staggered chicanes of Taffy Pull. The old woman was keeping it down to eighty, and he caught up in no time. Strobes but no siren he overtook her on her left, thinking to force her into her own lane, wondering if he could force her to do anything. He tried to think of an intervention tactic that left her any chance for survival.

She'd cranked up the volume. He could hear the singer taking on a drummer who might have been Krupa. In his dreamy state, Sergeant Kohlhardt heard the bawl of the engines recede, and the two cars were dancers moving across the floor.

A quarter mile ahead, floating above the road, was a pair of dim red dots. Eyeshine. Sergeant Kohlhardt blasted his air horn, flickered his brights.

The moose took up half the road.

The old woman floored it, and the big car surged as if snapping its leash.

Sergeant Kohlhardt, in the days that followed, for all the good it did, went on record in protest of the findings of the Minnesota Department of Public Safety's accident investigation, which concluded Beatrice Bernum, ninety-four, a Wisconsin resident driving under an expired license, mistook her accelerator for her brake. He furthermore filed a request for formal statement as to why the report omitted from its appendices all transcripts of interviews with responders at the scene, most specifically himself, as well as any and all references to *(a)* the car's make and year, *(b)* the elderly woman's scarcely creditable driving skill, *(c)* the blue flowers painted on the highway, and finally *(d)* his own expressed conviction that Bernum had with intent increased her speed and steered in to hit the bull moose.

Sergeant Kohlhardt did not make reference to his impression, in hindsight a flight of fancy no doubt, that *(e)* the moose stood dead center over the third blue flower as if waiting for her. ◆

R.D. GILES

FISH OUT OF WATER

IRIS WAS THINNING BEETS when a salesman appeared on the road, carrying a large sample case. She crawled through the dirt and pulled up seedlings by hand, trying not to damage rooted plants. As the girl worked her way down the row, she sang a hymn to the prophet. Iris had just finished the second grade and would soon be baptized by her father.

Dry farms extended in every direction, and a granite curtain of mountains enclosed the valley. The fields soaked up water from snow melt that filled jagged creeks high up in the pine and aspen stands and flowed down to the mouths of canyons and into canals and irrigation ditches. Inside Iris's clapboard house, her mother was preparing supper. The man from the road had stopped in front of the house and was now walking towards her, waving. He was not only the tallest, but also the skinniest man she'd ever seen. He almost seemed to be standing on stilts, and his wingtip shoes must have been twice the size of her father's boots. Iris could see he wasn't a Mormon; there was no temple garment under his shirt, and he wore a wrinkled suit with a filthy collar and no tie. His eyes were bloodshot, and he had a sour smell about him. The man tried to smile, but his lips drooped on one side.

"Are your folks home?"

"My mother is."

"I have something for you." He got down on one knee in a gangly motion and opened the sample case. Several bottles of wine tonic were strapped to the top, and his shabby belongings were stuffed in the bottom of the case. The man dug through his things until he found a pack of Black Jack gum. "Go ahead and take it. Tell your mom I'm selling medicine."

"Thank you," she said and ran back to the house.

Iris chewed a stick of gum as she washed up in the mudroom and changed out of her overalls into a dress. The kitchen was saturated with the smell of yeast rolls and beans stewing in suet and molasses, but Mother wasn't there. Iris set the table with the family's chipped dishes and mismatched spoons. She looked out the kitchen window and saw that the salesman was on the porch talking to her mother. He'd moved a pot of violets to make room for his case and was displaying bottles of tonic on Father's wooden chair. Iris came out to hear the sales pitch. The crown of the man's hat was almost touching the roof of the porch as he went on about how this one was "guaranteed to cure rheumatism" and another was for "dyspepsia." Behind him the sun was dropping over a mountainside pockmarked with copper mines. Mother reached into her apron when the man finished his pitch and gave him two coins for a bottle of New Life tonic. The apron was tight on her stomach.

"You should come in for supper," Mother said.

The salesman followed them in, stooping through the doorway. Iris's father and her brother Joe had just turned off the highway in a rickety Ford pickup and were driving the quarter mile or so down the dirt road to the house. They left behind a shroud of dust that hung in the air and spread over stalks of wheat and alfalfa adjoining the road. The truck bed was rattling with five-gallon milk cans as they pulled into the drive.

Mother had put the tonic away in the cupboard, and Iris was setting another place at the table for the salesman. He waited in the parlor, looking at a framed print that hung over the mantle. It was one of those pictures of the Savior with fair, shoulder-length hair parted in the middle and a forked beard. When father and Joe came in, the towering salesman introduced himself as "Bill."

They all shook hands awkwardly and followed mother to the kitchen, where a kerosene lamp illuminated the floral wallpaper. Iris brought a pitcher of cold water and set it in the middle of the table. The rolls were piled up in a basket, and mother filled everyone's bowl from a cast iron pot. When she took off her apron and showed Bill where to sit, he could barely fit his spindly legs under the table. Scowling, father folded his arms, indicating it was time for Joe to say the blessing. Iris and her mother sat down and bowed their heads.

"Our Heavenly Father, we ask Thee to bless this food that it will nourish and strengthen our bodies." Iris peeked to see what Bill was doing and caught him with his eyes wide open and his elbows on the table. Joe finished the prayer "in the name of Jesus Christ," and Bill went after the rolls, his long fingers moving across the table like the legs of an enormous spider, buttering and devouring them. When he started in on the stew, his skin turned sallow and sweat glistened on his forehead.

Father ate slowly and didn't say a word, but looked hard at Mother like he was asking why she'd spent good money on this man's alcoholic "medicine" when their growing family was living in a broken-down house and barely getting by on rented land. Why, his look said, did she keep inviting in gentile tramps whenever they happened to be in town or at a church meeting—or that time when he and Joe went out in the freezing rain to repair a fence, and both of them came back shivering, only to find a silver-haired Indian with a tubercular cough sitting by the fireplace. Father stayed quiet, but on his face was a look of dismay like he was remembering another time when mother kept three sparrow chicks hidden in a hat box and fed them worms she'd dug up under a rock.

"You got family around here?" Father asked.

"It was just me and my sister. But she died at the canning plant."

Everyone kept eating.

"They've had so many accidents," Father said after some time had passed.

"Me and her were working on a filling machine and taking leaky cans up to the top floor," Bill said. "We were both tired and all wet with brine. They got a freight elevator and I told her to use it. When she pulled the cable, there was a short, and she couldn't let go. I shut off the power but it was too late."

"They should've fixed that short," Father said.

"She was still like a kid. I used to take her to the picture show. Her favorite was the 'Baby Burlesks.'"

"You did what you could. I heard a fellow got electrocuted pulling someone off a wire at the sugar beet mill."

"I don't know," Bill said in a faraway voice. Neither of them spoke for a while.

"Where you headed?" Father asked.

"Nevada. I got a friend working on the new dam."

"I'm sure they'll have work for a big fellow like you."

"My friend says they got work for everybody."

"You might as well stay the night. We can set you up in the cellar."

Mother got up to put things away. It seemed like Bill was about to excuse himself from the table, but something was wrong. A blank expression had come over him, and he was grinding his teeth and picking at his shirt like there was hair stuck to it. His body stiffened in the chair, and he clenched both hands as his knees started banging against the table. The dishes and silverware rattled, and Father and Joe were about to pull away the table, but soon enough the salesman's legs stopped jerking. He managed to stand up and, teetering on his gigantic feet, braced himself against the wall.

"How can we help you?" Mother asked.

Bill staggered over to where he'd left his sample case in the hallway. He knelt down and unfastened the latch, his hands trembling. He took out a bottle of tonic that had already been opened, uncorked it and drank what was left.

"This one's for my convulsions," Bill said, slurring his words a little. "So I don't end up flopping around like a fish out of water."

Iris followed her parents around as they got the fruit cellar ready for Bill. Mother brought a wool blanket, and Father had Joe fetch a jug of water, a bale of straw and the lantern they kept in the barn. Bill crept down the steps, crouched over, dragging the case behind him. Father said a short prayer for healing, shut the cellar door and locked him in for the night. He promised to give the salesman a ride to the train station first thing in the morning and told Joe to pour out the wine tonic Mother had purchased.

Iris got into bed and chewed the remaining sticks of Black Jack, hiding each wad under the mattress when the licorice flavor was gone. Father didn't approve of her chewing gum. She stayed awake wondering if Bill would ever make it to the new dam in Nevada. Her teacher had said it would be the biggest one ever made, and Bill could help them build a giant wall to hold in all that water. Iris pictured him locked up in the cellar, lying next to burlap sacks of potatoes and dry beans, surrounded by hundreds of quarts of her mother's preserves lined up on shelves made of cinderblocks and salvaged boards. It was all in preparation for harder times to come in these latter days, and the great calamities that awaited in the end times when the Savior was promised to return. The lantern would be hanging from a nail, casting shadows over the straw where Bill would be curled up, trying to make himself fit in this cramped space. And what if he didn't have enough of his medicine to make it through the night? He might wake up and have nothing to drink but a jug of water and the other tonics for rheumatism and dyspepsia. Before long he'd be stricken with the worst kind of convulsions, thrashing around on the floor and knocking over glass jars of apricots and beets, biting his tongue and gasping for air. Iris worried that he would die alone down there.

Once, when the family was visiting relatives in Parleys Canyon, her brother caught a big rainbow trout and left it on the bank of an ice-cold stream for a long time until its movements were reduced to twitches of the head and tail, the bloody flap over its gills opening and closing, sand caked onto its shiny scales, the hook still attached to its mouth, one eye dim and glassy. Iris fell asleep thinking about the fish and dreamed that Bill was being baptized, wearing all white, plugging his nose as Father pushed his head under. When she woke up and went to look for him, the door to the fruit cellar was open, and the salesman was gone. ◆

MARY ANN SAMYN

FINALIST FOR THE LAUX/MILLAR POETRY PRIZE

EVERYTHING FILTERED THROUGH SOMETHING ELSE

Not quite the end, the main characters swim in the ocean.
It's after dark. Fifty pages to go. A reprieve.
How did Camus know to do that?
Most days, edges overlap, so I guess this is still the middle.
Or a thing reverberates a long time and grows famous.
I'm used to, but not quite over, what hurt me.
At the cemetery, I water the flowers, clip the grass and weeds.
The reason to make art is to be yourself before it's too late.
What do you hope to remember from the experience?
I don't want contentment to be out of the question.

SONYA SCHNEIDER
FINALIST FOR THE LAUX/MILLAR POETRY PRIZE

STAND BY ME

I don't remember the first time I watched the movie.
Probably in the living room of our crowded house

while my brother slept tucked against his bed rail.
I watched it so many times, I can, even now, close my eyes

and tell you every dusty piece of clothing each boy
wore, or the timing of the train as it barreled down the tracks.

I loved River Phoenix best, whose blue eyes and sad
smile lit the dark forest. When he found leeches on his bare skin,

I longed to kiss his blood-stained body, and when Gordie
stared down into the dead boy's half-gone face, I felt

the permanence of the find, like the first crimson stain
on my underwear. Only now, thirty years later, can I take in

the whole picture: I'm in front of the TV, pining
after these child-men as they wander the wilderness,

while my brother lies still, his face a muddled
moon glowing from a darkened room.

JOHN MULCARE

FINALIST FOR THE LAUX/MILLAR POETRY PRIZE

TRIMMING BACK APPLE BRANCHES IN OREGON

We were city kids working weekends in
an apple orchard. We heaved
hay with our too-weak arms, swept
the chicken coop clean of shit.
Afterward, we'd stand smoking,
watching the two palominos fenced
behind the thin wire on the property's
outskirts. We were always afraid
to approach them, and when we did
we frightened them, so we admired
them, and just how still they stood
in spring's half-thawed out slop.
When we walked between the apple
trees we'd spent winter pruning down,
balancing on top of turned-over buckets,
my friend stopped when he saw
the beginnings of blossoms on each
branch, and he began to weep. Looking
into those smudges of color, I don't know
what he saw or felt, if it was anything
like the first pangs of beauty beyond
speech I felt inside my body when I learned
how delicate something can be as I watched
a horse nestle its head into the torso
of another. I don't know if he also felt
undone by that. I touched his shoulder
the way I thumb the soft spot of an apple's
bruise. And he stood there, not speaking,
staring right past the trunks of apple trees,
through the wire fencing, at the two horses,

and the mountain range behind them, into
the sky cradling a future he decided couldn't be
approached. Not how we had. Not harshly.

ANDREW PAYTON

WINNER OF THE LAUX/MILLAR POETRY PRIZE

DESCALZO

My toddler removes his shoes
at every threshold

and Don Tonio warns
bare feet bring cold

but the child is off
into the garden, and Don Tonio

who has no legs
says that once he walked

all day in orchards above town
or this is what I hear

as Don Tonio has no teeth
and I have imperfect Spanish.

I came home tired,
he says, or I imagine

and I add,
It is good to be tired after hard work

and he agrees.
We are a family of sorts—

I carried him after mass
at his daughter's wedding

in my arms,
near to weightless

but these are memories
we both will lose.

On the television
an American superstar performs

for millions
and Don Tonio asks how much

for a ticket to the Super Bowl.
I google and say a number in dollars

and everyone laughs
and he asks about snow in Virginia

and I say less and less.
Somewhere in the middle of life

I too confront the impossibility
of ordinary dreams.

My children return
covered in red earth.

The garden rises behind
the couch where we sit—

palm and lime and lily rise
into the night sky

endless and naked.
I take the children by their wrists

to soap and scrub their faces,
their hands, their feet.

KRISTIN OFFILER

IF YOU CHOOSE A LIFE OF FAKERY

HE SAID HIS NAME WAS ELVIS, and I only went along with it because I told him my name was Cleopatra.

"Well, Miss Cleo," he said, leaning in close enough for me to smell the sweet stench of tequila and ginger beer on his mouth, "what does my fortune say?"

"Wrong Cleo, honey," I said, lacing my voice with sugar. You just never know with men how a correction might land. "But I can read your palm."

He stuck his left hand out slow as molasses. I wasn't even half as drunk as him, but I played at being toasted. For the performance.

"How many kids am I gonna have?"

I unfurled his fingers and studied his palm, noted the callus at the base of his ring finger and guessed like always. When your eye is trained to notice signs of life, you see them with ease.

"Says here you already have a kid. Or two?" I glanced up. His eyes went wide, then filled with tears. There it was; I pressed the tender spot further. "You miss them. And her. This line shows your heart, and I can see that it was broken but will mend."

"Shit," he muttered as he pulled his hand back, flexing it before balling it into a fist in his lap. "Did you go to school for that?"

"I learned it from my grandmother, like most things." I tipped some wine into my mouth. It was cheap but fine. "So what's that broken heart line all about?"

He groaned and dropped his head forward. His shoulders slumped, straining against his blue t-shirt. I wasn't necessarily attracted to him, but after scanning the hotel bar, he'd been the one my eye kept landing on. Late thirties I guessed, dark stubble on his cheeks, a weathered look around his eyes. Fractured just enough.

"I just know there's a story there," I said.

You always get the backstory first. Always. Understand a wound and it becomes your tool.

"Well, Cleo, it's a long story." He drained his drink and exhaled deeply.

"I've got nowhere to be," I said.

This was true and also false. But Gran had instilled in me all her wisdom, and the first thing I'd learned was that two things could be true at once. You could be both a good person and a bad one. A happy person and a sad one. You could be simultaneously wanted for larceny in one state while actively trying to steal from another person in a different state. Humans were complex. Women especially.

"You ever go through a divorce?" Elvis asked. "Anybody ever walk out on you? I bet the answer is no. Just look at you. Who would leave you? Are you married? No, actually, don't answer that."

He started to cry again, and I set my hand on his back. His body heaved under my palm, grief and resentment burning hot just under the surface.

"I've been left," I lied. "You wouldn't even believe how awful it was. Or maybe you would. Maybe we have our pain in common."

He blew his nose into a damp drink napkin. The square of paper tore against the force, and the bartender gave him a sideward glance, thick with judgment.

"She was sleeping with her friend's husband," he said. "You believe that? She would go over for book club once a month, and they would meet up afterward at the neighborhood clubhouse."

"That's terrible," I said. But even terrible stories could be ordinary, and bad spouses were nothing special.

"Her friend told me. His wife. She followed her husband this last time. Thought it was weird, right? How he's always going off for a beer run right as book club ends. So she followed him. Left their three kids alone in the house to do it. They were asleep, don't worry. Plus, they have a dog. But she found them on the tennis court. Can you imagine? Finding your husband balls deep in your neighbor—your friend—on a dark tennis court? Minutes after you hosted her, fed her, gave her wine?"

I rubbed his back some more.

"You poor thing," I said. "That's the ultimate betrayal."

"She came right to my house," he said. "Immediately. Parked her minivan in the middle of the road. Pounded on the front door. I ran down expecting the police saying someone was dead. But it was just the friend. Makeup streaked all over her face. Screaming at me, 'Did you know? Did you know?' and all I could do was stare like a fool."

"Shit. What a mess."

"Yeah. Then my wife comes flying in. Book club husband comes in next. Everyone is screaming. I'm in the middle of it all like a clown trying to make sense. Did this happen at book club? No, on the tennis court, the wife says. She shoves my wife hard, knocks her into the banister. I get in the middle, then the husband pushes me, and I'm seeing red. It's starting to make sense, sink in. My kids wake up. They're at the top of the stairs crying." He stopped to wave at the bartender for a refill. "Fucking shit show."

"I could sense the heartbreak cut deep, but I had no idea it was like that," I said.

He nodded gravely. I pulled back, second-guessing Elvis here. Gran always said to be careful for the ones who are too fragile. They're riskier. You had to find one with the exact right amount of pain in them. Not too fresh, not too old. You can only use the hurt at the right stage of fermentation, she'd say. Men never go to therapy, Gran told me once. They almost all have a usable weak spot somewhere.

"When did this all happen?" I asked.

"Last month," he said.

"Ah."

Then he turned and something changed in his face. The sadness turned to hunger. I knew the look. I was familiar with greedy eyes, a lustful mouth. He was transmuting his heartache. Energy couldn't be destroyed, after all. Just transformed. Sometimes it didn't matter if the hurt was still raw just as long as it could be reimagined for a little while.

"I'm staying here," I said with a nod toward the lobby. "You two still sharing a house?"

"I sleep in the basement," he said. "But I'd rather stay here."

"Come on, then," I said.

I handed the bartender my card to close out both tabs, and when I got up to leave, he followed. He was wordless in the elevator, but kept his eyes locked with mine between slow blinks.

"You want revenge," I told him as the elevator doors opened. "It's radiating off you."

This, for a change, wasn't a lie.

"I want to go back in time," he said. "I'd cut off his dick before he could use it."

"But she hurt you, too."

He shook his head. "Trust me. He's to blame."

This sweet, dumb man. We turned left off the elevator. My room was at the end of the hallway next to the stairs, as always, because I requested it that way. There aren't any elevators that can move as fast as my legs taking me away from a man whose valuables I'd just snatched. Or from a man who wanted more than I cared to give. You've gotta be able to move, Gran always said. Number one rule. If you're gonna take from people, body or soul or wallet, your skinny, no-meat legs better take you outta there faster than a cheetah. She bought me cheetah print socks when I was twelve just to make the point. Move your little ass quick.

I swiped my room card and pushed the door open. The air was artificially cold inside, just one bedside light casting a line of amber across the dark floor.

"Did you see this on my palm?" he asked with a humorless laugh as he untied his shoes and kicked them aside. "Did it predict you were going to take a sad sack back to your room?"

I put my purse in the closet, took off my earrings and necklace one by one. It was all so domestic, like we had been doing this for a decade.

"The palmistry stuff is open to interpretation," I said.

He squinted at me, undid his pants, let them drop to the floor. "What does that mean? Did you interpret this?"

I shrugged. His boxers were plaid. I hadn't expected that, and somehow it made me feel sorry for him. His wife had probably bought them for him in a multi-pack while she was at Target, maybe while texting her lover. Or maybe not. I had to be careful about assuming the worst of another woman solely based on the word of one heartsick man.

He stood there in his shirt and underwear and socks like he didn't know what to do next. His body hunched a bit forward, his belly pooched over the waistband of his boxers.

"You're a little drunk," I said. "Maybe you just need to talk tonight. Or sleep this off. You'll feel better in the morning."

"There's no sleeping this kind of thing off," he said. "Trust me. I've tried sleeping it off, drinking it off, running it off. It's always there. I can't get rid of it. Can you tell from my hand how long it'll last? When will I wake up and not feel like shit?"

He took a few steps forward and held out his palm. I gave it a cursory glance.

"You're still processing. That takes time, you know?"

"But what do the lines say?" He jutted his hand out again, firmer this time. It was such a human thing, a need for answers.

I pretended to examine the cracks along his skin. It wasn't that I didn't believe in palmistry. I did, a little bit. I thought anything mystical, anything a person was desperate enough to believe, had at least some merit.

"I can see that eventually you'll feel better once the score has been evened," I said. "Or at least once you feel like it's been evened."

He pulled his hand away from me and scratched at his belly where the waistband dug into his skin. I stared at the red elastic impression on his flesh, that stamp of vulnerability. And against my better judgment, it made me sad.

"Look," I said. This was a first for me. "I have to be honest. I brought you up here to rob you. Plain and simple. You were an easy target."

After a few seconds, his face split in laughter. He couldn't stop, couldn't catch his breath. He hunched over, hands on his knees, as he laughed and laughed. I inched away from him the longer it went on, positive that I'd miscalculated my move and said something that had caused him to snap. I didn't need to get bludgeoned with the lamp.

Finally, he lifted his face to me and wiped his eyes.

"Goddamn, that was funny," he said. "This is just my luck. I try to screw a stranger to get back at my wife, and I nearly get robbed. This is exactly my luck. Exactly."

I started to say I was sorry when he held up a hand to stop me.

"Maybe you can do something else for me?" he suggested as he stuffed his legs back into his pants and buttoned them. "Would you make a phone call?"

GRAN HAD BEEN A CHURCH-GOER ALL HER LIFE, just never the same church. It was an easy way to find a lot of people fast. We'd move to a new town every six months or so, depending on how quickly things fell apart. She always said it was wise to get out while the gettin' was good, citing the time she'd messed up and fallen in real love with a man named Walter, waiting too long to move us on. I was fourteen then, and we stayed a full year right up to the weekend of their wedding.

"It's pain now or it's pain later," she said. Her wedding to Walter was the next day, and she was teetering on the edge of making the worst choice. She paced the kitchen of our filthy little apartment. "Either we scoot now, or he finds out about me later. And either way, hon, it's bad news."

We scooted. Running was our thing. Packing up quick, getting into the car, vanishing like ghosts.

I couldn't drive yet, but I took the wheel when her sobbing got to be too much. She couldn't see a damn thing, she said, pulling the car off the road and getting out. Her eyes puffed up red hot like she had rubbed them with poison ivy. I'd never seen her so upset before, so untethered. It scared me to think a beating heart could cause so much trouble.

"You paying attention, Pearl? You see how wrecked I am? This is what not to do. I want you to remember this day and promise you won't ever be as dumb as your Gran," she told me that night in the dark of our hotel room. From my bed, I listened to her cry herself to sleep. Once she was out, I stole a cigarette from her purse and smoked it on the front steps. That was the best learning of my life, that sadness of hers. I went to sleep that night smelling smoke on my clothes and feeling steel in my heart.

We analyzed her missteps while we found the next place to settle down. Her first mistake was choosing a man who had lost his wife to death. He was too soft, too easy to love. Her second mistake was not keeping her feelings in check, letting them run the show like that. Her third was believing this time could be different, that she could stay put with her fake name, fake history, fake everything and he would never figure her out. She liked to say if you choose a life of fakery, be ready to have nothing real.

She was my whole world, the sun and every planet and the entire starry sky. But after I saw that even she could be a fool sometimes, I grew into a careful, crafty woman. Smarter than her in many ways, too.

Even still, I admired her willingness to snap her own heart in half before anyone else could do it to her. You don't see that kind of courage often.

ELVIS WAS BACK IN HIS CLOTHES and sitting on the saggy corner of my hotel bed.

"She told me I was worthless," he said. "That no one would ever want to be with me again."

"That's not up to her."

He held his cell phone out to me, his wife's name already on the screen. One button to push and I'd be able to give this poor guy an invaluable gift: a tiny shred of revenge.

"You're sure about this?" I asked. He nodded and I pushed the icon for a video call. It was well past midnight, so I almost didn't believe it when she answered.

"Caleb? Is that you?" she said, scruffy with sleep. She was all shadow on the screen. The phone's microphone made a scratchy sound as it rubbed against bedsheets.

"You can call me Cleo," I said. "Caleb's right here with me. In my hotel room. We just wanted to say hi, sweetie. How's your night going? As fun as ours?"

I could see her eyes bugging even in the dark. Could hear her voice sputtering like a car that wouldn't turn over.

"What the hell is this? Caleb? What are you *thinking?*"

"We're not doing much thinking," I said and laughed.

I knelt down and held the phone out so we were both in frame. She blinked several times, rapid-fire furious, and I felt a tingle of satisfaction at the back of my neck.

"What'd you have for dinner, Sandy? Cereal again? And did you take the kids to play tennis after?" he asked. "We drank at the hotel bar. I ate steak, then we came up here for dessert."

I couldn't help but whip my head to look at him at the sound of his voice. So icy, so perfectly calculated. He grinned at her with the devil in his eyes, and I thought, this is not the man who just stood in front of me in boxers looking like a hairy, pale potato. No, no.

"Jesus, you're a piece of shit, Caleb. Have fun with your whore."

Then, three beeps after she hung up, we both fell into a fit of laughter. He rolled back on the bed, hiccupping, chest heaving. I stood beside him, unable to stop my own giggles. How often did I laugh like this? Almost never. I was always too busy plotting my next move to ever pause and savor a moment this purely.

He sat back up, and I just knew he wasn't the same Elvis from earlier anymore. Maybe never would be again. No turning back once you cross a certain line.

"Shit," I murmured. "That was fun."

"I haven't felt this good in a long time," he said as he rubbed his forehead. "A long time."

I thought of Gran and Walter. Of her foolishness and missteps. And knew I was tripping straight into my own set of mistakes this very night with this stranger. I should've been satisfied just lifting his wallet and disappearing out the fire exit while he slept. I should've been scooting out of there ASAP, leaving no trace but the ghost smell of my perfume in the air, but instead, I settled in next to him on the mattress, and our vengeful laughter rang all night. ◆

ANNE ELLIOTT
THE OTHER REDHEAD

NOBODY COMES TO THE COOLER to see me. They don't come for poetry. They come for the other redhead, the one with the tiny waist and large feathers. There's always the other redhead.

I sat at the bar in my taffeta thrift store prom dress, crinolines mounding around me, twenty-dollar ukulele in my lap, strip of red drink tickets in my hand. My set was done, so I drank something with a cherry. Here, the poets needed props—a ukulele wins a crowd, but not like the act that followed me. All eyeballs fixed themselves on the other redhead. The drummer brushed his snare; the redhead brushed her bare leg with the tip of her blue-feathered fan. Her hair was a slow, shiny curl over one eye. Her lips, matte scarlet, pursed into a valentine, and her shaped brows popped in mock surprise. Kick drum, heartbeat, sparkly stiletto heels. She showed the dimples of her backside, glittery g-string between powdered cheeks, then unshowed it with a sweep of the fan, peeking over her shoulder. "Ooh!" she exclaimed, and hipsters laughed, and her hips pivoted, slow and confident, to the drummer's va-va-voom.

Finally, in profile under bright spotlight, she lifted both fans, arched her back, tilted back her head, closed her crisp-lined eyes, let the world look at her small, even bosom, her blue sequined pasties, her naked waist, the s-curve of her behind in profile, as her red curls cascaded down her back. Her skin—all of her skin—was porcelain. Beside me, a man put fingers to lips for a whistle.

Poetry could not stand up to this person. Not even with a ukulele.

I snapped fingers in applause with my free hand, the one that wasn't drinking. She earned it. I could never be as brave as that red-haired girl. I could scream private and profane thoughts into a microphone—I could confess, I could rant, I could sing even though I couldn't sing, I could play ukulele even though I couldn't play ukulele, I could be the fool for the room to laugh at—or with—the dumb bunny with the brash voice, the girl who would yell anything as long as there was funny to be found. But I could never do what that woman did. I am the other kind of red-haired girl, the kind who wears a sweatshirt at the beach. Under the taffeta dress was an old-world girdle, all bones and shaming panels, the only way the dress would zip up. I had been holding my breath for hours.

I felt a hand on my back and smelled the old-man cologne of the evening's host. "Do you think you could give us another number?" he wet-whispered in my ear. He was younger than me, but dressed like a cartoon gangster from my father's era, hair tall with Vitalis, gray sharkskin suit crisp. "Mazzy didn't show up, and Lovely Miss Blue needs two minutes, maybe five, for the costume change into her balloon number."

"I've started drinking," I said. "I'm in no shape."

"I've been drinking since four PM," he replied. "You think these people care?"

That was a very good question. What *did* they care about? Why *did* they come here? To taste the meats of the Meatpacking District? To laugh at a girl with a ukulele?

Or to whistle at a girl with nearly nothing on?

"Okay," I said, because that is what performers say.

"You're a doll," he said, pinching the bones of my girdle. *Doll* is not what people call me. I loved him for it. I hated him for it. "Hunky dory," he said.

My waist ached. I schlepped my ukulele to the stage. The host, in a sudden, lively Bronx patois, prompted a loud round of applause for the other red-haired girl. Then me. Such impatient faces in the front. I plugged in my ukulele and sighed into the square metal microphone, then closed my eyes to make the hornball in the front row disappear.

I had planned a silly ditty, but it escaped me, and I crooned instead an old ballad, one I did not even write, one that made me cry when I watched skinny Audrey Hepburn save the ginger cat. Silly songs need sobriety, open eyes, watching the crowd for cues. But not this one. My father taught me to play it decades ago, demonstrating on the small frets with his big fingers. Eyes still closed, I made my awful voice as sweet as I could muster, raspy and earnest.

The drummer joined in, as if the whole thing were planned, with a gentle brushed waltz. I wanted to kiss him. I whistled an extra verse. The ukulele sounded true, for once. Maybe I was not a clown at all.

The song ended, and I bent at the waist to bow. Applause was thin. Quiet enough to hear the rip of my vintage dress, straight down the zipper stitching, exposing the satin of my old-world girdle. I felt the blush from my cheeks to my ears, the tight dress going slack. The drummer could see my underwear. I didn't dare walk back to the bar.

The host wanted another number. "Miss Blue is not ready yet!" He stage-whispered, rolling his palm to signal: keep going. "Just one more?"

I looked up at the old stainless hooks hanging from the ceiling. Before this place was a bar, those hooks suspended the chilled carcasses of cows. "Well," I said into the mic. "Now I can breathe. You would not believe this girdle." Did they laugh this way at Ethel Merman? Did she ever play The Cooler? My next number was a complaint about calories, because what else would you yell about after bursting through your formalwear? Lovely Miss Blue, pale and nearly naked, stood breathless in the wing.

It takes this long to change from naked to naked?

I sang. It would be over soon. I bellowed. A few of the hipsters laughed.

As I exited the stage, the drummer tossed me something: his white dress shirt, damp with his sweat. He shrugged and smiled, stripped down to his plain white tee shirt, armpits circled with perspiration. I nodded a thank-you and pulled the shirt on over my mess of a dress. The audience did not notice. They were looking at the girl wearing nothing but blue balloons. Part of me was grateful to be invisible. The other part filled with bile at the sight of her.

New drink tickets awaited at the bar. I put them to use. Now that I could inhale, the medicine went down easy.

DRINK TICKETS SPENT, still thirsty, I decided to escape to a cheaper bar, one where I wouldn't be asked to fill dead time with numbers no burlesque audience wants. Around the corner was a Meatpacking institution, a bar festooned with bras donated by women desperate for drink.

I might be a woman desperate for drink. "Do you take girdles?" I asked the barkeep, though I wouldn't be giving up mine. Without it, no part of this dress fit. I sipped Pabst Blue Ribbon and looked up at the hundreds of bras hanging from the light fixtures. Most of them were overstretched, gray from too many washes. The strategy, perhaps: bring the bra worth less than the beer.

But perhaps the donation of a bra to the rafters of this famous bar was not an economic decision. It was not, perhaps, even an artistic decision. I waited, nibbling gross nuts from a shared dish, for a woman to make a trade so I could analyze her motive. The men all around eyeballed the barmaids, who played along with exhausted expressions, smiling and offering glimpses of tight-tied aprons and well-built backsides in countrified jeans. The wrong kind of country blasted from the jukebox. The cheapest beer was not worth this price. I swigged down the remainder of mine and started to put my coat back on.

But then I spied the drummer chatting with the bouncer. He spotted me immediately and walked over with a grin. "Miss Maggie Martin!" he said, and stood at the bar next to me. "What, you're leaving?"

"You know my name, but I don't know yours."

"Clarence," he said, holding out his hand for a shake. I took it. Someone behind me shoved, and I was suddenly in the face of Clarence, whose shirt I wore shamelessly under this jacket. I felt my heart quicken, so close to his face, saw the shadow of stubble and the long curl of his pretty eyelashes. I let myself hold his hand longer than a handshake. The beer made me brave.

"Get Miss Maggie one more," said Clarence, my new hero. I let go of his hand so he could pay the barkeep. Was there a ruse to grab his hand again? Did I even need one? *He gave you his shirt,* I reminded myself.

He smiled and handed me a new beer. I let the foam coat my lip, then licked it off. "Thanks for the shirt. You saved my bacon. Are you freezing? Do you need it back now?"

"That wouldn't quite be gentlemanly," he said. With a sly smile, he handed me a business card. "Call me. We can work it out." *Clarence Fisk, percussion,* with a picture of two drumsticks in the corner.

"Where are your drums?" I asked, fingering the tip of the drumstick poking from the breast pocket of his jacket.

"In the van. I told Claudine I would meet her here."

"Claudine?"

And all the male heads turned to look at the new meat entering the bar: a young, pale, petite woman wearing a black knit beanie over glossy, curled red hair. Her—the other redhead. Lovely Miss Blue, fully covered now, but impossible to hide the shaped auburn arches of her eyebrows, her skin still flaked with glitter. The drummer waved two fingers, and she pushed her way through the groping crowd, greeting him with a kiss on the lips. Clarence and Claudine. Claudine and Clarence. Of course.

She turned to look at me. "'Moon River.' I love that song," she said. Her voice was much deeper than I expected.

"Thanks." Imagine, thinking I might have a chance with this man, just because he lent me a shirt. "Then I had to go and ruin it by ripping my dress."

She gripped my shoulder in a familial way. "Are you kidding? You would not believe the wardrobe malfunctions I have had. You just gotta laugh it off. You were an old pro." She looked me in the eye. She was a person, not a doll at all. "You just grab the room with your voice. I wish I could do what you do."

"Shout useless poems at people who aren't listening? Sing with this fucked up voice?" My father used to tell me I was prettier when I wasn't talking. *Just a little friendly advice,* he said. If I wanted to find a husband, better to smile than to speak. *What if I don't want one?* was my response. *Oh, you will,* he said.

"Well, I was listening to you," Claudine said. "How did you get into that? Poetry?"

"Blowing off steam at open mics." Yelling at someone. Yelling at my father, who was too dead to hear it. Saying what I could have said when I was too busy smiling pretty. But Claudine's smile seemed genuine, full of gums and goodwill. I wanted to hate her, but I couldn't. "Felt like bitching at people while drinking beer," I said.

"I heard that," she said. "I need some beer. Then I'll start bitching." Claudine looked up at the desperate bras, suspended wardrobe malfunctions like so many cold carcasses. Clarence looked for the bartender. "I wish I could do what you do," Claudine said. "Spoken word. Using your voice. *Screaming.* I love your guts."

Guts so big they burst through my clothes. But the other redhead had bigger guts, big enough to leave the clothes backstage. Maybe I was supposed to reciprocate, but I didn't wish I did what she did. "How did you get into that?" I say. "Burlesque?"

She shrugged. "Some girlfriends and I wanted some kind of feminist sex-positive expression. Don't always turn out that way, though," she said, with a brief shudder.

"Like when the host calls you Doll?"

"And the other things they call me," she said under her breath.

Clarence pulled Miss Blue close to him, seemed to be sending a message to the rest of the bar: this girl would not be paying for drinks with her dingy underthings, and she would not be going home with anybody but him. And then I noticed something else, in the set of her jaw. She was afraid. Not of Clarence. She side-eyed the pack of wallet-chained hipsters at a nearby table, some of whom I recognized from The Cooler. They recognized her too, if not me. A predatory leer shaded their gaze as they pretended to talk to each other. Claudine was afraid in this bar—afraid in a way that I was not.

I hadn't noticed just how deep my envy was of her—until that envy swallowed itself in this thirsty crowd. Behind Claudine's back, a stranger reached over and twirled a curl of her glossy hair around his finger. She didn't notice. Clarence didn't either.

I shot the guy a glare, and he glared right back, before returning his hand to his pocket. *Don't you wish I wanted to touch your hair?* said his expression.

Pretty can go fuck itself, said mine.

I was no longer thirsty. I just wanted something to eat.

I thanked Clarence for the beer and the shirt, bowed to both of them and made my exit.

ON THE WAY TO THE TRAIN, I stopped in the all-night bagel shop for an everything with schmear. Three drag queens—endlessly tall in their lady trappings, tottering on stilettos—stood at the counter and sized me up while I ordered those calories I did not need. There was no hiding the disdain in their painted faces. As I left, I heard one of them remark sotto voce, "Such a shame. With a little attention, she'd be such a lovely girl."

Lovely: fat lot of good that is.

Girl: no safety for you in this city.

Attention: somehow, always, the wrong kind, from the wrong person.

"Pretty can go fuck itself," I said—aloud, this time—to the pretty queens.

THE E TRAIN PLATFORM WAS DESERTED, then the train car. It was two AM. I should have been afraid but was too drunk. I sat on the stained subway seat and let the crinolines heap, rested my ukulele in my lap and flopped my head on it. The wheels rocked me to sleep. My friends always nagged me not to sleep on the train, but I couldn't help it.

I woke up, as always, just as the train pulled into my stop in Queens. Along the way, as always, the seats had filled with restaurant workers in their checkered pants, ragged copies of El Diario on their laps. All men, but I wasn't scared. They did not even see me.

All but this one. He sat directly across from me. His gray hair was styled like Sinatra, and he wore a wool coat, too heavy for the season. He looked right at me with dark eyes and a pained smile. He reminded me of my father, gazing over his newspaper with concern, the way one looks at a lost girl.

I felt a cold jerk in my gut, as the door beside me opened. The jerk of being found out.

"Are you okay?" said the man.

I straightened my spine. I stood and smiled pretty. "I'm hunky dory," I replied, stepping into my station. ◆

ALICIA REBECCA MYERS

PARKED CAR

I don't have much time to write this poem, Yankee game on the radio, you on the soccer field in the purple evening light, it turns the jowls of a Plott hound into a Renaissance fresco, windows lowered, a freshness permeates the air, hard to think that glacial worms exist, that your new best friend's father is a recent widower, I touch with gratitude the bruises on my wrist from where our puppy mouthed me, I brought him to my last therapy session, another screwup to talk about next week, lucky I am still here, why am I still here, why do some pennies get pressed into commemoration, the pitch is high, I have hardly any time to write, about thanks and arbitrariness, what gets tossed and what elongated, to tell the elusive world I love it, to put away my phone as you fling open the door, in the sudden dusk your knee bloody

TYLER KLINE

CONTAINER STUDY

The summer rain didn't work & neither did reheating the tenders in the air fryer
or the last silo in November. Walking the lake counting turtles on logs
did nothing. Same for crying in the car wash. Neither did the ghost emoji.
My father grew disgusted buying Shakespeare all those live mice.
Followed the forecast to the point where I was believing I was part of the forecast.
The bassist said think about dying. That did & then it didn't work.
My mother's obsession with throw pillows. Validated. Pulling the red string
that sticks out of the wall that keeps going & going throughout my life.
I couldn't stop buying tulips & throwing them down wells. The number
32 & its green cloud energy wasn't helping. Deleted the app that tracks
how many lantern flies you squish. I'm sorry. I don't know what I was thinking
that summer nothing worked. I made up new lives in my favorite fields.
Turned inward like a towel tucked into a swan on a budget line cruise ship.

LESSON ONE

Before paying for the groceries, my father said *Oh and this*
which was my cue to hold up what was left of the apple.

The woman smiled, typed in a number. On the drive
home, my father let me pick the station. I couldn't decide

between rock or classic rock, so he reached over and pressed *TAPE*.
I knew nothing about potential. But the motivational speaker

made it sound like something you could dig up from the dirt
alone in the woods behind your house with your blue Walkman.

It was the age I first desired exactness. Years later, a doctor
would suggest leaving a piece of trash on the floor of my car

each day until the end of the week, then write down
how it made me feel. I lasted until Tuesday, then tossed

the used tissue at a stoplight on Butler. Lesson one ended
with the tape saying it was all about grit. Never any luck.

Even when a song came on that he loved, my father never
sang to the radio. I imagined he had a beautiful voice.

RACHEL MORGAN

POSSIBILITY

On a long walk, I sit under a roof
of long-standing oaks. A book
by a forester claims trees talk to trees.
What cartographers couldn't see
they sketched as evil sea beasties,
here be, here be. The spectrum
of visible light is narrow. I try
not to be sad for what isn't.
This morning's news broadcasts
the morse code talk of stressed
thirsty tomato plants.

Just think of every discovery
announced after our lifetimes.
Wouldn't we like to visit
for one dappled afternoon,
reading the marvelous headlines?
Trees have perfect childhoods.
Trace your DNA to its star of origin.

Explorers returned with exotics—
bright feathers, orchids, a spice
that tastes like butterflies look.
Later, in my son's pocket, I find
his collection—a dingy feather,
gravel, wood chips from the playground—
his tiny revelations are a lantern,
illuminating what I've forgotten how to see.

LOIS MARIE HARROD

AT THIS POINT GRIEF BOOMERANGS

I am just trotting down the street
minding my busyness—

red stiletto to the shin—
no stopping to say *oh, so surly.*

*

Or I'm wildebeesting
from the Serengeti to Masai Mara

and a crocodile jaws my hock
and I begin limping towards the riverbank

when a lion rushes the grass
to gnaw out my heart

*

Or I pick up James Joyce's *Ulysses*
filled with your cramped scribbles—

no Rosetta Stone to translate
the glyphs.

*

And this old shopping list—
did you scrawl *gouda or gone?*

DAWN A. FULLER
CLICK CLACK

SOME YEARS AGO, our neighbor got married for a second time in the house where she lived. Even though we didn't know her, we were invited to the wedding.

The groom was Italian, and his father, from the old country, reminded us of Dad's best friend, Alex. I think he was a farmer like Alex. Maybe not. Maybe he did construction. Either way, his skin was warm and brown from being in the sun, and his hands were calloused. He wore scuffed working man's boots, dress polyester pants, and an ornate polished belt buckle—reserved for special occasions. He sat near us on his own. In his clipped accent, he thanked us for coming. His small, comforting smile felt like being back in the Imperial Valley amongst farm folk loading sugar beet trucks together until the sun went down. It was as if we'd known him all our lives. He pointed frequently, telling us with no sound to "Eat. Eat."

The bride's father wore a tailored gray suit that was shiny, and so was his gray, slicked-back hair. His skin was red. He looked hot. His teeth were white and long. He made sure to get around to all the guests to introduce himself, shake hands too hard, and tell us that he owned this house, not his daughter.

During the wedding, the groom played the piano. I wasn't sure he knew how to play. The keys were in the same two notes. He sang a song he wrote for his new bride on their special day.

"Then things were gettin' bad, really really bad ..." didn't seem like wedding lyrics to me. Then, just like that, some happy things happened in the song. When you weren't expecting it, suddenly he turned back to, "Then things were really bad, they were really really bad."

The singing itself was so bad that I looked around nervously. My mouth was dry. I waited to see if anyone else was getting as red in the face as me. He sang for ten minutes. Maybe fifteen. Dad had to go outside after three. I was in shock, and so was Mama. The bride leaned on the piano with her hands propped under her chin. She cried and dabbed her eyes with a tissue.

We left early.

A few months after the wedding, there were late-night SUV peel-outs down the driveway that her father owned. There was occasional shouting. They packed up the SUV and went to Burning Man. Neighbors said the new bride had been spending time down at the local swimming pool wearing a pink thong bikini and spiky high heels while she walked the edge of the pool with click clack balls like we had as kids in the 70s, clacking.

The happy-sad, singing Italian husband moved away. We never saw the Alex lookalike father we liked so well again.

They got a divorce.

Late one summer night, when the moon was out and everyone was asleep, the SUV peeled out of that driveway for the very last time.

It's been years now.

Boyfriends peel out every now and then. Sometimes they leave skid marks.

Yesterday, a red monster truck pulling a tall red crane carefully turned our street corner. After much maneuvering, it pulled up to the pool click clacker's house. The crane cranked high high into the sky. Once it was fully extended, a giant hook behind the trailer hitch started creaking. It lifted an almighty hot tub up into the air above the house. All the neighbors came out to stare with hands on their hips, or shading their eyes from the sun.

We stood there watching. Waiting.

When the fuss was over, we all went back inside. Mama said, "Why did everyone have to go and watch that? Who cares."

I played the air piano and sang the wedding song. It felt good. I guess it wasn't so bad. It was kind of sweet.

I wonder where the Italian father is, and I wonder if the gray, shiny father knows his daughter put a hot tub in his backyard; maybe he owns that, too. I wonder, will she do the click clack balls around the hot tub in the backyard now? I wonder, will we hear about a new wedding or a new delivery, or hear an SUV screeching down the road?

I just wonder.

Click clack. Click clack. ◆

KATIE BURGESS

THE COMPANION

THERE WAS NO CHANCE OF SKIPPING our weekend with Dad, not once Hurricane Cayleigh got downgraded to a tropical storm. By the time she neared the Panhandle all that was left was wind and rain, enough to blow down the neighbors' Christmas decorations but not so much that we'd have to shelter in place. Mom told us to pack our bags and stop complaining.

"Look," she said, "maybe try telling him honestly how you feel about—everything. He does care about you both, and I know he wants your visits to be a positive experience."

Mom only ever referred to awkward, difficult things as "positive experiences." Family therapy, canvassing for long-shot political candidates, me getting my first period while out canvassing for said candidates, etc.

Ollie sat methodically wrapping cords for his phone, his Switch, his iPad, placing each item in the appropriate case. I dumped the tangle of objects from my nightstand into my backpack, then started grabbing books from the living room shelves. I chose *Moby Dick, Bleak House,* and *Anna Karenina,* not because I liked or even understood all that nineteenth-century prose, but because they were the longest books Mom owned and would take up any time I might otherwise have to spend interacting with Dad and Bethany.

Back then I also sometimes imagined I might be a secret genius if I made a real effort. I pictured myself casually handing all three books back to Mom on Sunday, saying, "These were *fascinating*—do you by any chance have *War and Peace?* I thought I might squeeze it in before winter break ends." And she'd call the high school and berate them for never challenging her precious daughter Charlotte enough and demand that I be put in honors with Ollie.

"Planning to read all that in three days?" Ollie said. He dropped his bag on the sofa and plopped down next to it.

"I'm being prepared," I said. "Dad might ban screentime again."

"So we'll point out the irony of *him* accusing us of spending too much time on our devices."

Mom closed her eyes. She was doing one of her mindfulness exercises, touching her thumb to each of her fingertips while inhaling and exhaling slowly. We'd overheard her talking to friends about Bethany after our last visit. Apparently the lawyer said she could claim Dad wasn't properly monitoring our media content, but only if Bethany said or did something inappropriate in front of us. Otherwise, there was no way to restrict her presence.

Ollie and I fidgeted and stared at our phones until we heard Dad's car in the driveway.

"Oh my god," Ollie said, looking out the window. "He brought her with him."

I turned my head. There Bethany was, staring vacantly out the passenger window, her bare feet propped up on the dashboard.

Ollie threw up his hands. "We can't go two hours without having to see his sexbot?"

Dad objected to the term "sexbot," and insisted that Bethany did, too, as if her thoughts weren't part of her factory settings.

"This is why you should let us drive ourselves," Ollie said. "They wouldn't pull us over as long as we went the speed limit. And we wouldn't have to ride in the car with *that*."

Mom ignored this, as she did all of Ollie's arguments about how a learner's permit was basically a license. She closed her eyes and touched her thumb to her fingertips again, so forcefully that her knuckles turned white. I wondered if mindfulness could break a finger. Then she ushered us outside, where Dad stood holding his Florida Gators umbrella.

"Happy holidays," he said.

"Really?" Mom said, gesturing at Bethany.

Bethany's hair was red this time. Her pouty lips parted in a way that was probably meant to be seductive but always looked more like she had a cold and couldn't breathe through her nose.

Dad shrugged. "I got to use the HOV lane."

OLLIE AND I LAUGHED our heads off at the first ads for LuxeDolls, never imagining that one day we'd be expected to sip mocktails and play Monopoly with one.

"Hi, I'm Krystal. And I want to be with you in every way," said a platinum blonde robot in the most famous of those ads, the one parodied on all the late-night shows. Krystal wore a modest lace nightgown and lay on a bed strewn with roses. Cut to Krystal doing crossword puzzles, sitting in a fancy restaurant, and singing a lullaby to two small children.

"Krystal looks like a princess!" said the littlest child.

"LuxeDolls," said the voice-over. "For Total Luxury Companionship. Now with Just4Fun, SexxxyTime, and KidSafe modes."

Years later, in my college sociology class, we watched a docuseries, *American Dolls,* about the LuxeDoll phenomenon. It was uneven, but it covered some things I'd never heard about, like Cherry Laurel, Florida, the planned community for people in LuxeDoll partnerships. It wasn't far from Dad's place in Green Pond, so I was surprised he hadn't moved there, but then again Dad was philosophically opposed to any place with a homeowners association.

It was pouring once we got to Dad's townhouse. He tossed Ollie the keys so we could hurry inside while he wrangled Bethany out of the car, but the brief dash from the driveway to the front door was still enough for us to get soaked. I went straight to my room and grabbed a towel for my hair. I was digging out dry clothes when Dad called our names.

"Hey, I thought we could do a Christmas movie marathon after dinner," he said once we opened our doors. "Pop some popcorn, get in the spirit?"

"Um, I have a lot of homework," I said, gesturing at my pile of giant novels.

"Me too," Ollie said. "I have, like, three papers to write."

"You don't go back to school for two weeks. How much homework could you possibly need to do *tonight?*" Dad asked, an edge creeping into his voice. "All we have is this weekend, and I've got the parade in the morning. You're not holing up in your rooms tonight."

Thunder rumbled outside. I tried to think of a homework assignment that couldn't wait until after the holidays. Some kind of science experiment? Something I had to observe and write notes on each night? I was drawing a blank. Ollie rolled his eyes and sighed.

"Great!" Dad said, giving a fist pump.

AFTER DINNER Dad broke out all the classic movie snacks: popcorn, Junior Mints, Twizzlers. He set instant cocoa and four Christmas mugs on the coffee table. Bethany slouched on the sofa, clutching a bag of popcorn in one of her French-manicured hands. Dad had dressed her in a fleece reindeer onesie, complete with antlers. I assumed he was going for cute and festive, but the effect was more like a sexy/evil horned sorceress from one of Ollie's RPGs.

Dad plugged in his electric teakettle and plopped down next to Bethany. "Who wants hot cocoa? Babe?"

I heard the faint whirring sound that always preceded Bethany talking. "No thank you," she said. "You're all the sugar I need."

Ollie turned and stalked into the kitchen. He came back with two insulated paper cups and handed one to me.

"Let's get through this positive experience," he whispered.

We each emptied packets of cocoa into our cups and poured in hot water. I sat in Dad's recliner, as far away from Bethany as possible. Ollie grabbed a sofa cushion and sat on the floor next to me.

"She's in KidSafe Mode, for crying out loud," Dad said. "It's the same as hanging out with your mom and Robert."

"Not. The. Same," Ollie said.

Truthfully, we were also weirded out by Mom's boyfriend Robert, who had a sad ponytail and lied about being able to speak Japanese, but at least we'd never accidentally found his genitals in the dishwasher.

If Dad heard Ollie's comment, he ignored it. "What should we start with—*Home Alone? Elf? A Christmas Story?*"

"Gee, I don't know," Ollie said. "Bethany, what do you think?"

Bethany blinked. "There are so many choices! I'll let you pick!" she said. Only her lower lip moved when she spoke, and it didn't match up with what she was saying. It was like a hand puppet controlled by a little kid, all random flapping.

"Fantastic," Ollie said. "Who wants a partner with opinions, right?"

"That's unfair," Dad said. "Bethany has all kinds of opinions. Don't you, Babe?"

"I have all kinds of opinions," Bethany repeated. "I enjoy fine dining as well as SEC football, and I especially love boats!"

"Wow, you're right, Dad," Ollie said. "She really has layers. Boats, you say?"

"I vote for *Home Alone*," I said. I hated *A Christmas Story*, and we always watched *Elf* with Mom. I had no feelings one way or the other about *Home Alone*, which made it perfect.

Ollie kept going, though. "Look how uncomfortable Charlotte is. Are you fine with your only daughter thinking that women can be replaced with objects?"

I wished we actually had that telepathic link that twins were supposed to have, so I could tell Ollie to shut up, that there was no point in having this conversation again. But no, Ollie always thought I needed him to speak for me. I tried to look away, but then my eyes landed on Bethany's boobs, and all I could think about was how Dad had picked them out. He'd scrolled through a menu of hundreds—thousands?—of possible boobs, maybe agonizing over the decision. The nipples were so pointy you could see them through the bulky fleece.

Dad muted the TV and looked at us. "I want Charlotte to be as content as I am. I want both of you to find what works for you, and to feel free to live your lives however you want and not be ashamed of it." He held up his hands as if challenging Ollie to argue with any of that.

"Everyone should feel free," Bethany said. "After all, this is America, isn't it?"

"Well put, Hon," Dad said, "Now. We have one vote for *Home Alone*, which I'll second. All in favor?"

"Aye!" said Bethany.

THAT NIGHT I SAT in bed and scrolled through pictures of friends on their winter breaks. Some had gone skiing. Some were taking last-minute beach trips now that Cayleigh had subsided. Everyone grinned in their selfies, as if to say, "Look at me, having an amazing time with my family members, who are all human beings!"

I had a few likes on my last post, a video of a plastic snowman that had blown into a neighbor's pool and appeared to be drowning. Mae, who'd been my best friend in ninth grade but who I didn't see as much now that she'd switched to a charter school, had commented with a laughing face. I sent her a picture of an axolotl, and she sent one back. She messaged me: *"how's your dad's robot girlfriend? does she want you to call her mom?"*

I tiptoed out to the den. Dad had fallen asleep on Bethany's shoulder, his mouth hanging open. The TV was still on, its glow casting giant antler shadows on the wall behind them. I took a few pictures, until I got one that made the shadows look the most ominous, and I sent it to Mae. In less than a second, she responded with a cry-laughing axolotl.

Could I have guessed what was going to happen? *American Dolls* had an episode on scandals involving LuxeDolls, but it barely mentioned the whole thing with Dad, only throwing in a few headlines as part of a montage. Brief outrage over one local news anchor wasn't much of a story compared to a senator leaving his wife for a LuxeDoll, or a wellness influencer using one to babysit her toddler. It felt like a big deal at the time, though.

THE NEXT MORNING, Dad and Bethany had on matching bathrobes at the kitchen table. Bethany was giving the weather report.

"Seventy degrees with eighty percent humidity," Dad said, shaking his head. "That's a Florida Christmas for you."

"The *way* you spend Christmas is far more important than how much. Henry David Thoreau," Bethany replied.

"Isn't that great? I downloaded a famous quotes pack so she can edu-cate me. There's coffee and biscuits ready." He squinted at us. "Do you kids drink coffee yet?"

We each put a biscuit on a napkin and sat at the table. I tried reading *Moby Dick* as I ate. I kept rereading the first page, unable to process it, but its bulk was still an effective barrier between me and Bethany.

As I reached for my biscuit, though, my hand brushed against Betha-ny's, and I jumped.

I knew about the innovations in RealSkin™ thanks to the ads. It used some mineral—I can never remember the name of it—the one that was killing all those midwestern miners until the EPA banned it. Combined with silica stone, it produced an unbelievably soft texture. It felt real yet not real—so perfect, so smooth. I felt my own hands, and they felt like troll hands in comparison. My hands, with their lines and veins and fine little hairs. Their calluses from gripping my pencil too hard. I took a breath and turned my focus back to *Moby Dick*.

"That's some pretty advanced reading. Is that for school?" Dad said.

I nodded.

"Hey, I've got an idea," he said, holding up his iPad. "I'll upload the text to Bethany's knowledge bank, and she can quiz you on it. You'll be ahead of your whole class."

"No, that's okay," I said. "That might be considered cheating, I think."

"I don't see how," Dad said. "And I can add anything else, too, like discussion questions and articles. She's about to become a literature ex-pert." He fluttered his fingers the way he did whenever he mentioned anything he considered fancy—literature, opera, tiny dogs. He tapped an icon, and we watched the progress bar change from gray to green. "There! Check this out—Bethany, what are the major themes of *Moby Dick?*"

Bethany blinked and tilted her head. "Moby—touches on many themes, including fate, revenge, religion, and man versus nature. An-other theme is madness, as seen in Captain Ahab's obsession with killing Moby—the white whale."

Dad frowned. "She seems to be hiccuping a little."

"Moby—also explores the concept of free will as an illusion," Bethany continued.

"Oh my god," Ollie said, putting his hands to his mouth. "She can't say 'dick.' She's in KidSafe Mode, so she can't say the word 'dick.'"

"What? It's in the *title*," Dad said, messing with the app some more. "Okay, let's try again, Beth. What's the name of the whale?"

Dad kept trying, but she wouldn't utter the word. He looked at his watch and muttered to himself. "I need to head downtown," he said. "Sure you don't want to come watch the parade?"

"We're sure," Ollie said.

The station always sent Dad to cover the Green Pond Christmas parade, basically a couple of middle school bands, city council members driving classic cars, and a too-skinny Santa on a tractor. Ollie and I used to go for the candy they tossed out, but even that was mediocre.

"Suit yourselves," Dad said, heading to his room to change.

"Hey, Bethany," Ollie said, "what's a nickname for 'Richard'?"

"Rich, Rick, Ricky, Rico," Bethany offered.

"Not any of those," Ollie said, "there's another one I'm trying to think of."

Dad emerged a few minutes later dressed in a gray suit and candy cane tie. "I'll bring home dinner," he said. "Shouldn't be more than a few hours."

"Those hours will feel like an eternity to me," Bethany said.

"Aw, Honey," Dad said. He kissed her on the cheek, then took a cord from a drawer and plugged it into her back. "Don't everybody get too bored without me."

"I would rather die of passion than of boredom," Bethany said. "Émile Zola."

I SPENT THE MORNING in my room, trying again to read any of the books I'd brought. Eventually I gave up on being a secret genius and went back to scrolling aimlessly on my phone. I stopped when I noticed my picture of Dad and Bethany—Mae had posted it. It had over a hundred likes. I didn't know how I felt about her sharing it without asking. Then again, there was no caption, nothing connecting it to me. And it was nice to have a new inside joke with Mae—it had been a while. I commented with a vomit face and moved on.

Ollie knocked on my door.

"You have to come see this," he called.

Ollie couldn't stop giggling as I followed him back to where Bethany sat. On the kitchen TV, Dad was exclaiming over preschoolers doing a baton routine to "Jingle Bell Rock." The rain had stopped, but the sky was still overcast, making it look almost like nighttime. "Aren't these little ladies adorable!" he kept saying.

"Watch," Ollie said, barely containing the giggles. He turned to Bethany. "So, Bethany, tell us the meaning of life."

"To brave these fearsome billows is meaning enough," Bethany said.

I shrugged. "What does that mean?"

"Don't you recognize the style of your new favorite book?" Ollie said. "The one you've definitely been reading all day? Bethany, can you expand on that?"

Bethany's eyes darted back and forth. "Men possess delusions that invest every happenstance with divine mystery."

Ollie held up Dad's iPad. "He never changes his passwords. She knows all of Herman Melville now. And nothing else. I deleted the rest of her knowledge bank."

"*All* of it? Even—?" I couldn't bring myself to utter the phrase "SexxxyTime mode."

"It's perfect. She loves boats, remember?"

As she kept talking, I couldn't tell what was a real quote and what was a jumbled-up imitation. Occasionally she'd throw in a "Call me Ishmael," which I recognized from my extensive study of *Moby Dick's* first page, but the rest sounded like nautical gibberish.

"Bethany, describe your perfect date," Ollie said.

"Hoist the powder pans upon the forecastle!" she said. "For the lord of the Leviathans is a moody captain."

"So true," said Ollie. "So true."

DAD CAME BACK THAT AFTERNOON with a glazed ham and sides from the gourmet grocery store near his complex. There was sparkling cider for Ollie and me. He put on a Christmas jazz playlist and hummed as he poured a glass of wine for himself and another for Bethany. We always watched but could never pinpoint the moments when he managed to drink from her glass, only noticing how her wine would gradually disappear. We sat by candlelight.

"So how's everything been over here?" Dad asked, serving his plate and then Bethany's.

Ollie passed me a paper plate. "Fine. Bethany, what've *you* been doing with *your* day?"

I slid down in my seat, wondering if I should go ahead and clarify that I had nothing to do with Bethany's new personality.

"I try all things. I achieve what I can," she said.

Dad cut into his turkey. "That's a great attitude to have, Babe."

Ollie and I looked at each other. What if he didn't even notice?

"I mostly did homework," I said.

Dad frowned. "It seems like that school is giving you a lot of work. I know it's supposed to be pretty advanced, but if they're piling too much on you, I'm happy to talk to them. You gotta take a break sometime, right?"

"'Think not' is my eleventh commandment, and 'sleep when you can' is my twelfth," Bethany said.

Dad laughed and slapped the table. "You know what, that's great. That could go on a T-shirt or something. Babe, say that again!" Bethany complied, and he laughed even harder. "That's incredible. The rate at which she learns—she starts with basic phrases, but then her conversation gets more and more sophisticated." He patted her hand. "That's the amazing thing—you interact enough with this—I don't even like to call it *artificial* intelligence. Because what is intelligence if not the ability to synthesize information and transform it?"

Bethany's wine glass was empty.

"That's really deep, Dad," Ollie deadpanned as Dad refilled his and Bethany's glasses. "Bethany, do you have any deep thoughts to share?"

"On board the whaling ship, the sailor fights daily against the killing madness," she said, her voice disconcertingly cheerful.

Dad frowned for a second and then laughed. "Oh, your book got uploaded after all—did you get a chance to let her quiz you?"

I relaxed. Maybe Dad would assume it was all his own doing. Maybe he didn't even care what words came out of Bethany's mouth.

"A little," I said.

"That's great, sweetheart, I hope it was useful." Dad started clearing plates. "Should we watch *Home Alone II* while we have our dessert?"

"At last there will be merriment, like laughter at a funeral, a jest as a balm to calamity," Bethany said in a rush, as if, having gotten used to talking like discount Melville, she was really getting into it.

WE WERE OPENING PRESENTS—checks for us and ceramic bowls we'd made in art class for Dad—when Dad's phone rang.

"Why is work calling me?" he mumbled. He answered, and then his voice quickly became more tense. He stood and walked into the kitchen.

"What do you think that's about?" asked Ollie.

"The sea, the sea," Bethany said. "The mighty, tumultuous sea."

When Dad came back in, his face was red. "Do you have any idea why I got that call?"

"Because of the sea?" Ollie said.

Dad held up his phone. "Who did this?"

It was the picture I'd taken, but it wasn't on Mae's profile. The photo was paired with a clip of Dad at the parade, saying how adorable the baton twirlers were. Put into this new context, it looked like Dad was leering at the little girls. It had already garnered thousands of angry faces.

"Well?" Dad said. "Did one of you take a picture of me while I was sleeping and send it to some organization called Moms for Decency? Because I don't know who else could have done it. And my boss is not amused."

"The shipmates must have their amusements," Bethany piped up, "or else they sink into idleness and vice."

It turned out Mae's mom had seen her post and grilled her about it, then spent all day tracking down details about Dad, until she found the parade footage.

"This man has his SEX TOY out in front of his own children. Do you really want him that close to your daughters?" said the caption in a video posted by the Moms group. That inspired complaints to the station about having Dad assigned to a "family" event.

Dad spent most of the evening in his room, on the phone with his boss, his coworkers, and, once she heard about it, Mom. We occasionally heard bits of conversations: *My life is my business. Nothing is even going on in that photo. Name one thing I did that was inappropriate.*

"So," Ollie said, "you sat there saying nothing all last night, and then you put our weird family shit out there for the whole world to see."

"I only sent it to Mae."

"And I don't know if it's okay to take pictures of a sleeping person."

"How am I the problematic one now?"

Bethany tilted her head toward me. "An exceedingly problematical character," she chirped.

Dad eventually came back. "I'm sure you probably thought it was funny. But you could have caused some real problems. Thankfully I think it's going to blow over." He must have figured out the source of the photo, because he was looking right at me. Sure enough, he continued, "Charlotte, honey, if you were uncomfortable around Bethany, you could have talked to me."

"Um, I seem to recall expressing lots of discomfort, and you didn't care," Ollie said.

"I'm sorry you feel that way," Dad said.

"Sorry I *feel* that way?"

I slid down in the recliner, fiddling with the upholstery buttons. I wanted to apologize, and I also wanted to say I regretted nothing. I couldn't say what I meant, because I didn't know what that was, as if I had my own erased knowledge bank.

THAT NIGHT I WAS DRIFTING off when I heard shouting. In my half-asleep state I couldn't make it all out: Something, something *disrespect,* something something, *take a joke.* I rolled out of bed, eased my door open, and looked down the dark hallway. Then I heard another voice—Bethany, in a breathy moan, repeating the same lines over and over: "I stab at thee! I stab at thee! From Hell's heart I stab at thee!"

So Ollie had in fact tampered with SexxyTime mode.

"Come on!" Ollie was saying. "It's funny!"

Dad turned and saw me. "Do you think this is funny, too? Go ahead, laugh."

"I would prefer not to," Bethany moaned.

"Have I not been trying my best?" Dad said, rubbing his temples. "Have I not done everything to make everybody happy this weekend?"

"I'll show you how to set her back," Ollie said. But Dad slammed the door in his face.

Dad was wrong about everything blowing over. Mae had deleted her post, but people found the archived version. They noticed my vomit emoji comment and speculated about whether my father's creepiness was negatively impacting my mental health or whether I was kink-shaming. By that afternoon the *Green Pond Observer* had posted an editorial that didn't mention Dad by name but was full of statistics about the porn industry's influence on girls' self-esteem. I switched all my profiles to private, but not before my DMs filled up with requests for comments, messages of support, and criticism of my looks.

The weird thing was, when the station finally called to suggest it was best if Dad resigned, he was suddenly calm. He sat wordlessly for a few minutes. Then he cleared his throat.

"The sun's out," he said. "Let's go ice skating."

The city set up an artificial ice rink every winter. None of us skated well—Dad couldn't go more than three feet without falling over and cursing so loud I worried they'd make us leave. But it was a relief to have something to do, making our uneven circles on that big block of polymer. We stayed out there for hours, until it was time for him to take us back to Mom's. It's one of the images that sticks out the most to me from that weekend—the bright blue sky and his clumsy, laborious skating. He looked so vulnerable.

It wasn't long before he got a new job with a morning radio show that was psyched to use his minor controversy for ratings. He got his own segment where he discussed current events with two LuxeDolls, Mandy and Jessi. His catchphrase was, "She can make me a sandwich!" It was hugely popular with angry men, as well as the Moms for Decency, who listened carefully to each episode so they could complain about it in their videos. Dad often reminded us that he was only doing a character. But sometimes I would glimpse something in him, like his eyes or his laughter seemed just a tiny bit meaner than they used to, and I would wonder if he thought I should be making some guy somewhere a sandwich.

Mom was able to make him put Bethany away during our visits from them on. A few years later he upgraded to one of the LuxeDolls that could stand and walk, and after she knocked him off his back deck, permanently damaging his shoulder, he dated a series of real-life women who had less personality than a LuxeDoll. That sounds judgmental, but, as Ollie always pointed out, at least Bethany read some books.

I wonder what he did with Bethany—I know from the documentary that her generation of dolls can't be recycled. Did he resell her? Throw her away? Despite everything, the idea of that makes me sad. I don't want to think of her stuffed in a closet somewhere, or lying all smashed up in a landfill. Without battery power, can she sense it if a part of her is broken? Are all the words she knew still there in her knowledge bank? I prefer to think that she's still running somehow, that somewhere, she is dreaming of the sea.◆

MERCEDES LAWRY

WINTER RELENTLESS

Winter's bony fingers
nettle and wither.
The blunt sky evokes absence.
The branches of the apple tree
imply turmoil, with no purpose.
It is light we all seek
despite ourselves, thickened
with ennui, not as glamorous
as a listless beauty in a French film,
rather, heavy with undone tasks,
so mundane, so fiercely necessary.

COMMON COUPLE

The trespass is hollow,
perhaps a mockery.
The pinched woman steps back
as if observing, testing.
The man in subtle agony
soundless, while she
breathes, measured huffs
of sour air. She dared
or he did, impossible
to tell. The broken glass
at the periphery of damage.
The end in sight.

ALEXANDER ETHERIDGE

SILENT QUESTION

—after W.S. Merwin

It was a long time ago now
I was a boy
in a different life
sitting on my grandmother's porch
staring out at the trees
always staring through
the clear air of seasons
at two towering white elms

They were distant
so I loved them more
I felt they were part of
another world
another age

I could watch for hours their
branches waving calmly in breezes

They asked for
nothing nor answered
any question

except for the one I
knew there were no words for

DANIEL CHAN YEE ANN

AFTERWORD

We were paring back, becoming plainer, simpler
as in elementary level, or even Baby's First Reader,
large pictures for pages, sometimes a few words:
Bedspread. Beachball. Sweater. Swing Set. Lamp Cord.
Meanwhile, keeping at it, unable to up and drop
our lives altogether, we roleplayed as ourselves,
filled flutes of wine glasses with gold apple juice,
drew up to-do lists in the cool condensation,
watched clock hands crossover and join at the twelve
till the bar of new soap rounded down to a slippery pebble
and the sum of all words embossed and engraved
rinsed quietly out of our days, and then days, days,
                    the grand parade of them trooping
                    out of nothing towards the horizon.

PASSING THROUGH A GATE: POEMS, ESSAYS, AND TRANSLATIONS

JOHN BALABAN

COPPER CANYON PRESS, 2024
$24.00

BOOK REVIEW

ROB GREENE

THE POETRY SCHOOL OF EXPERIENCE REVISITED: *THE TRAVELER ISN'T LOOKING BACK, EVEN THOUGH WE WANT HIM TO.*

WHEN A POET SITS DOWN to finally write the poem that is meant to be written, after carrying lived experiences around for days, weeks, years, decades, the poem that is meant to appear on the page shall most often appear. At least, that's the hope. With some of us, there's no forcing the issue when it comes to material. Reading *Passing Through a Gate* by John Balaban, I had a sense that I was visiting the poet's past and anticipating an unwritten future. As someone who admires John Balaban's work, I look forward to the new poems that will follow this essential collection of poems, translations of primarily Vietnamese and Romanian poetry, and essays on translation and the writing life.

Here I'll disclose that John Balaban knows me, maybe better than my own family knows me, as he, together with Dorianne Laux, and Juliana Nfah-Abbenyi served on the thesis committee for my MFA at NC State University over a dozen years ago. These professors did not talk very much about themselves, but they did lead by example. My mentors taught me to be brave on the page and to write my way through emotionally laden moments from my past and present days. John Balaban was one of my more generous teachers. Like me, he wears his heart on his sleeve, occasionally speaking with a harsh clarity. For the purpose of this review, however, I stayed within the poems of this collection, allowing Balaban to be "vetted through poetry," a phrase borrowed from the book's eponymous essay "Passing Through a Gate."

In the poem, "Daddy out Hitchhiking at 3 a.m.," we first meet the "traveler" who we'll follow, in one form or another, throughout the book. In this poem, the weary one seems to be expecting his first child, on the run from his past. Just how far that past is away from the present leaves us all to wonder. Each section of the book opens with an effective epigraph. In a later section of the book, our "traveler" is still coming from the direction of his past, but now he's not looking back. Poems in the vein of his very powerful "Driving Back East with My Dad" derive from experiences prior to Balaban's time in Vietnam, which he has written about extensively.

In this one, as the speaker is driving East with his Father in his old pickup, we gain glimpses of how difficult his childhood was. In fact, after one too many "punch-ups" at home, the speaker ran away from home at sixteen. Yet Balaban's portrait of a harsh father in "Driving Back East with My Dad"—resembling his fierce yet rather remarkable Romanian-American father—includes room for redemption. As someone who has witnessed my family from Kyrgyzstan struggle to settle inside of America, coupled with my own difficult childhood experiences, I can relate to this poem from many angles. "Driving Back East with My Dad" was first published in *Great River Review* in Spring/Summer 2006, and then in Balaban's fifth book of poetry *Path, Crooked Path,* and it finds new resonance inside the pages of this curated volume—poems that convey empathy and understanding of our neighbors all over the globe deserve to be seen by as many as possible.

Which brings me to a discussion of what, exactly, makes an "essential" collection of John Balaban poetry. As a lifelong fan of his pre-war material, and given my own predilection for the poetry of experience—as against the poetry of the imagination or the maps of abstract thought so many today regard as cutting edge—I suppose I want to see the "traveler" pause and perhaps turnaround from his walk along the highway, to come inside the house for a moment and show us more of his beautiful yet difficult past. I want to get to know young John Balaban better, as someone who may have a lot in common with how he grew up. Reading *Passing Through a Gate* made me wish for more Balaban poems set within the schoolyards and the working class and rent-controlled and section-eight housing within the rural areas north of Philadelphia. I personally want to read poems that open the curtain further on the complexity of a writer's character.

This is not to deny the power and importance of Balaban's more well-known subject matters, including the war in Vietnam and Vietnamese culture. As a conscientious objector, John Balaban was drawn to learn the Vietnamese language and to serve humankind as a scholar, riding around the rice fields on his bicycle to ask five hundred or so Vietnamese individuals, one by one, to sing their favorite poems to him.

As someone who has studied the Russian language off and on for twenty-five years, I realize I am nowhere near close to mastery of the language. I very much admire anyone who has the ability and the drive to learn another language as an adult, especially for the purpose of fostering peace. Balaban's follow-through and grit as a conscientious objector show in the strength of his poems about that era: poems that touch on his boyhood friends nailing up forts in the old neighborhood, his young adulthood spent in Vietnam during the Tet Offensive, then back safely inside of America as a young protective father. Balaban's poem "Words for My Daughter" masterfully captures many lived experiences packaged all inside one work of poetry.

But beyond the humanitarian service he provided in the rescue of wounded children and the related poems he has provided us with, his work as a translator must be mentioned. Highlighted in *Passing Through a Gate* are his translations of poems such as "A Tiny Bird" that convey power with the repetition in phrases from the description of the bird to how many times the bird drinks up the lotus pond "day-by-day" before flying off one last time.

Balaban conducted poetry interviews with rural native Vietnamese people, using a hand-held recorder, often with the sounds of mortar fire in the background. Through this work, and the foundation he later established, he gave new life to the folklore poetry of an entire culture and ensured its digital future. He was one of the first to provide America and the larger world a lens through which to regard the everyday people of Vietnam as the beautiful, gentle citizens of the earth we now all know them to be. This is an example of empathy at its finest—empathy, as in, the ability to see through the eyes of the Other. It is surely one of the main tasks of the poet.

There is no rulebook for making an "essential collection," especially when it comes to a poet whose life has contained many chapters. This book from Copper Canyon will provide any reader with plenty of insight and inspiration. John Balaban has given the world and our society many contributions. Together with many others who have influenced me in life, John Balaban has personally had a role in helping me turn my life around, more than once. Perhaps, I don't want the dear traveler to leave our lotus pond until he looks back a little more. My only hope is there shall be more poems from my generous teacher. *Encore! Encore.* ◆

FROM THE PUBLISHER

AS WE APPROACH our fifteen-year anniversary at Raleigh Review, the magazine is changing direction *again*. We're used to changing course whenever we, as a team, believe we're going off the rails, I have welcomed those changes.

One project we are launching in the coming months for the magazine community called *Zine Alive Archive.* This project is for all those who have poured every ounce of themselves into their beloved magazines and who then had to stop publishing. After ceasing their publications, many boiled down and labeled those now closed magazines with one word and that is a downplay of the effort and the sacrifices made by all those involved. When the closing day eventually comes for a magazine, "defunct," doesn't tell any of the story of the life's work, the passions, nor does it respect the talent inside and behind every magazine that has to halt their publications for one reason or another. And that is why we're launching *Zine Alive Archive*, a forthcoming repository for those magazines that have had to close their publications.

Every sale of this magazine in your hands goes to pay for the next issue. Yes, the magazine began with me on my plug-and-play blogzine called *RIG Poetry* on 21 February 2010, all brewed inside my Raleigh home office during a metaphorical storm.

I turned the original ignition switch and placed the art first. The art came above my own standing or the self-aggrandizements and self-importance of anyone else.

Above all else, our talented team based all over the USA and around the globe is the reason this magazine is still here. I am now just a proud team member at *Raleigh Review.* The magazine has grown way beyond me as the lone initiator, the sole originator, the founder, the creator, a co-incorporator, the first proprietor (a master of this or that or whatever) all held up inside my Raleigh home with my growing family.

All I did was strike the match and then continuously breathed life into this magazine by putting the art first. With our team adding in talents and expertise over these fifteen years, *our* magazine is now its own entity, its very own being. Still, over the past few years, I have been forced to face my own mortality and it seems fitting that contributions to the field include helping to ensure all our magazines continue to be available for the generations to come. We thank you for supporting *us* as we work to promote accessible works of experience that convey empathy and understanding among our neighbors all over the globe. ◆

Rob Greene, publisher

contributors

DANIEL CHAN YEE ANN is a queer and disabled writer living in Singapore. His writing has been published or is forthcoming in *Hunger Mountain*, *Shot Glass Review*, and elsewhere. He gets by teaching part-time while tending to a chronic injury.

KATIE BURGESS lives near a mayonnaise factory in South Carolina. Her work has appeared in *McSweeney's Internet Tendency, New Orleans Review, The Rumpus,* and elsewhere. Read more at katieburgess.fun.

ANNE ELLIOTT is the author of *The Artstars: Stories* (Indiana University Press). Her fiction can also be found in *A Public Space, STORY, Crab Orchard Review, Ploughshares Solos, Witness, Bellevue Literary Review,* and others. She lives in Maine. Learn more at www.anneelliottstories.com.

ALEXANDER ETHERIDGE has been developing his poems and translations since 1998. His poems have been featured in *The Potomac Review, Museum of Americana, Ink Sac, Welter Journal, The Cafe Review, The Madrigal, Abridged Magazine, Susurrus Magazine, The Journal, Roi Faineant Press,* and many others. He was the winner of the Struck Match Poetry Prize in 1999 and a finalist for the Kingdoms in the Wild Poetry Prize in 2022. He is the author of *God Said Fire* and *Snowfire and Home.*

FLORA FIELD is a poet from Oregon. She received her MFA from Columbia University where she was a Teaching Fellow. Her poems can be found or are forthcoming in *Tupelo Quarterly, The Vassar Review,* and *LARB Quarterly.*

DAWN A. FULLER is a Hungarian American, award-winning fiction writer. The author of *A Dollar a Piece* (2017, Lady Blue Publishing), her work has been featured in *Adanna, Black Fox, Boyne Berries,* and more. She is currently completing her first full-length novel set in rural Missouri, *Hannibal: A Ghost Story,* along with her life's passion, *Tuomb Beoir (A Good Woman),* based on the remarkable lives of Irish Traveller women. She lives on the Central Coast of California.

TOM GILBOY lives and writes on Colorado's Front Range. Not counting several children's books about a turkey in a fez and an argyle sweater, this is his first published story.

R.D. GILES is from the Southwest and has also lived in Spain and Latin America. He is currently working on a collection of short stories. His recent creative work has appeared in *Flash Fiction Magazine* and *Tupelo Quarterly.* He is a veteran and teaches early Spanish literature at Indiana University.

ROB GREENE is the founder of *Raleigh Review,* and he is a father of four.

LOIS MARIE HARROD'S recent publications include her 18th poetry collection *Spat* (Finishing Line Press, 2021) and her chapbook *Woman* (Blue Lyra, 2020). Dodge poet, life-long educator and writer, she is published in literary journals and online ezines from *American Poetry Review* to *Zone 3.* More info and links to her online work are at www.loismarieharrod.org.

TYLER KLINE is a writer from Pennsylvania whose work has appeared or is forthcoming in *Best New Poets, Colorado Review, Denver Quarterly, The Massachusetts Review, Narrative,* and *Poetry Daily.* He recently earned his MFA at New York University where he was a Jan Gabrial Fellow.

MERCEDES LAWRY is the author of three chapbooks. Her collection, *Vestiges*, was published in late 2022 by Kelsay Books. Her new collection, *Small Measures*, is available from ELJ Editions. A Pushcart nominee, she's published poetry widely and received several awards. She also publishes short fiction.

DAFYDD MCVEIGH is a writer originally from suburban Indiana. He is currently an MFA student at the University of Illinois, Urbana-Champaign.

A faculty member at the University of North Carolina School of the Arts, JOSEPH MILLS has published several collections of poetry with Press 53, most recently *Bodies in Motion: Poems About Dance*.

RACHEL MORGAN is the author of the chapbook, *Honey & Blood, Blood & Honey* (Final Thursday Press, 2017), and her work appears in *Prairie Schooner, Alaska Quarterly Review, JAMA, Beloit Poetry Journal, Shenandoah*, and elsewhere. She is the winner of the 2020 Fineline contest. Currently she teaches at the University of Northern Iowa, edits for the *North American Review*, and is a 2025 Iowa Artist Fellow.

JOHN MULCARE is a poet from the Pacific Northwest. His poems have appeared or are forthcoming in *POETRY Magazine, Salt Hill Journal, Thrush Poetry Journal, The Hudson Review*, and *Northwest Review*. He lives and works as an electrician in Philadelphia.

ALICIA REBECCA MYERS'S poetry has appeared in publications including *Best New Poets, River Styx*, and *SixthFinch*. Her full-length manuscript, *Warble*, was chosen by former Kansas Poet Laureate Caryn Mirriam-Goldberg as the winner of the 2024 Birdy Poetry Prize (Meadowlark Press). She currently lives in upstate New York but grew up in Raleigh.

KRISTIN OFFILER holds an MFA from Lesley University. Her work has appeared in the *Waccamaw Literary Journal* and *The Bookends Review*, as well as *The Bookends Review Best of 2020* print anthology. Her debut novel, *The Housewarming*, is forthcoming from Thomas & Mercer. She lives in Rhode Island with her husband and young son. Connect with her on Instagram: @kristinoffilerwrites.

ANDREW PAYTON is a writer, learning designer, and climate advocate living in Harrisonburg, Virginia with his partner and children. His poetry is featured in *Denver Quarterly, New Ohio Review, Nimrod*, and elsewhere. He graduated with an MFA in Creative Writing and Environment from Iowa State University.

AMANDA RABADUEX is the author of the poetry collection, *Resin in the Milky Way* (Cathexis Northwest Press, 2024). She is the managing editor of Etruscan Press and an associate poetry editor at *West Trade Review*. Originally from Ohio, she lives near Knoxville, Tennessee, and can be found at amandarabaduex.com.

MARY ANN SAMYN is the author of seven collections of poetry, including *Air, Light, Dust, Shadow, Distance* (2018) and *The Return from Calvary* (forthcoming 2025), both from 42 Miles Press.

SONYA SCHNEIDER is a Northwest poet and playwright with San Diego roots. Her poetry can be found or is forthcoming in *Potomac Review, Moon City Review, Catamaran, Mom Egg Review, Naugatuck Literary Review, BODY*, and *SWWIM*, among others. She holds diplomas from Stanford University and Pacific University's MFA in Poetry.

Nominated for the National Book Award, the Eric Hoffer Book Award, and nominated three times for the Pulitzer Prize, J.R. SOLONCHE is the author of 38 books of poetry and coauthor of another. He lives in the Hudson Valley.

contributors cont.

KELLY TERWILLIGER is the author of two collections of poetry, *A Glimpse of Oranges* and *Riddle, Fish, Hook, Thorn, Key.* She works as an oral storyteller, teaching and performing with children and adults.

HAN VANDERHART is a queer writer living in Durham, North Carolina. The author of *Larks* (Ohio University Press, 2025) and *What Pecan Light* (Bull City Press, 2021), Han hosts *Of Poetry Podcast* and co-edits the poetry press River River Books with Amorak Huey.

Memorandum
To: Readers and Writers
From: HR

AGENDA:

HARVARD REVIEW

Fiction / Essays / Book Reviews / Poems
Art / New Translations / Conversations

SUBSCRIBE ONLINE / HARVARDREVIEW.ORG

COMING SPRING 2025

RALEIGH

vol. 15.1, Spring 2025

REVIEW

SUBSCRIBE TO RALEIGH REVIEW
FOR THE LATEST ISSUES!

www.ingramcontent.com/pod-product-compliance
Lightning Source LLC
Chambersburg PA
CBHW050350030726
47503CB00008B/2712